THE COCAINE ZOO

ANGHUS HOUVOURAS

SEVERED PRESS
HOBART TASMANIA

THE COCAINE ZOO

WWW.SEVEREDPRESS.COM

ISBN: 978-1-922551-67-2

CHAPTER ONE

Some would argue that torture is worse than death. Death is finite. Pain can last for what feels like an eternity. Ending a life is a quick, and often painless act. A bullet through the brain registers less feedback to your nervous system than a paper cut. Killing is an act of mercy. Torture, an act of carnage. Searing a man's flesh, exposing him to inhumane levels of sensory overload, watching a person having their humanity stripped away one brutal beating after another. Truly, there is no more heinous act.

Fernando Suarez had sat in that chair for eight days. The horrors unleashed upon him by his tormentors were the kind of unspeakable acts that could only be committed by Godless men. The kind who no longer concerned themselves with consequence. Who either no longer believed in damnation or no longer feared it.

In that chair, Suarez had been broken, in both body and spirit. This underground prison had been his home for two years. In that time, he spoke barely a word to his captors. This was due to a number of different circumstances. The first six months had been spent in complete isolation. The only human contact came from the sight of a hand sliding a tray of food through a slot in the door. The next six months saw the same routine repeated with the addition of a single sentence.

"Tell us everything you know, and I promise you will see the light."

Fernando Suarez would not bargain. He would not give up his associates. Even if it meant spending every remaining day in this disgusting squalor. There were principles to which he adhered and things that he feared more than his captors. More than isolation. More than suffering. Perhaps even more than death.

After enduring a long stint in a dark, damp hole, he was re-integrated into the population. While he was desperate for interaction and communication, he didn't recognize any of his fellow inmates. They were strangers to him. For all he knew, these could be the same men responsible for his capture in an elaborate ruse engineered to get information from him. Paranoia is a defense mechanism, and a damn good one. It shuts out all rational thought and eradicates trust. He was no more likely to speak in front of his fellow captives as he was to those cloaked in shadows offering release for his compliance.

With traditional methodology proving ineffective, they moved onto more direct techniques. Waterboarding. Electrocution. Beatings with blunt instruments. Creative dentistry. Threats to family and friends. Acts of unmentionable barbarity with unclean surgical instruments. And in spite of these horrific acts being perpetrated against him, he would not speak. His captors were running out of options leading to this marathon of savagery.

Each session was several hours in length with small breaks for cigarettes and mop buckets of water to clean the floor of blood, urine, and feces. They only took off their masks while indulging their vices, the room always hazy with a thick layer of acrid smoke. There was a casual attitude to their frequent breaks. The kind of water cooler conversations that one would indulge at a factory or an office. General banality of a life that seemed so far removed from this place. They sipped cheap liquor and every so often replaced the cigarettes with cigars. There was no pleasure in their work. It was a job. These weren't bloodthirsty sadists, but clock punching middle men.

"Sin valor," he said, spitting blood onto the floor.

"What's that mean?" asked Carl, lighting a cigarette.

"The worthless," replied Abe, uncapping a bottle of screw top tequila.

"Anger," he said, holding out an empty glass. "What would we have without it?"

"Let's find out," said Abe, stamping out his cigarette and pulling down his mask. The last of the smoke escaping through the mouth and eyeholes.

He returned to the chair where Fernando sat patiently waiting for whatever terror they would unleash next. His vision was blurry, the byproduct of swollen, blood filled eyes. But he could hear the plastic cooler scraping across the floor as Abe dragged it over.

"We've been doing this so long, Fernando," he said, opening the cooler. "I think I've spent more time here with you the past two years than I have with my own family."

Abe had a way of smiling after every sentence. An ear to ear grin that could only be glimpsed through his mask.

"Two years, Fernando. Most of the people we deal with are either broken or buried by this point.

But not you. You are a testament to the tenacity of the human spirit. The boys had been taking bets on just how long you'd last down here," he said, rooting around the cooler, moving his fingers through the ice.

"You beat even the most liberal estimate by fourteen months. Be proud, Fernando... be proud," he continued, producing a bottle of Coca-Cola and popping off the cap.

"To your health," he said, holding the bottle into the air and taking a sip.

"Plenty of men have walked out of here without spilling a single secret, but none of them are like you, Fernando. You're the cockroach who won't die no matter how many times you step on it. As a man who has spent his entire life trying to survive, I respect that. But it has to end today, one way or another."

There was a fluidity to the way Carl and Abe worked together. A rhythm they had achieved after years of wet work. The moment the cap came off the bottle, Carl circled behind Fernando, a pair of needle nose pliers in hand.

"I need to know the location of the factory, Fernando. And I need to know where it is today."

As soon as the period ended the sentence, Abe hit his next cue inserting the pliers into Fernando's nose, pulling one nostril open wide, stretching the skin to its maximum elasticity and plugging the other with his gloved thumb. At the exact same moment, Carl's thumb covered the top of the coke bottle to protect the contents as he whipped the bottle back and forth causing the contents to fizz and foam. Then, like clockwork, Carl removed his thumb from the bottle and inserted it into the open nostril as Abe pulled away the pliers, forming a seal. The carbonated contents erupted from the bottle up into Fernando's nasal cavity, pushing out the oxygen from around his brain. His body spasmed, and within a second of release he had voided his bowels, bladder, and the contents of his stomach. After several seconds of agonizing pain, Abe removed his gloved thumb allowing air to circulate. They were the sweetest breaths Fernando Suarez had ever taken.

"They call it a brain punch," said Carl, filling up a bucket. "It's unpleasant, I know. And to be honest a bit beneath me."

He struggled for breath, sucking down air in gulps and gasps.

"I take no joy in this, but I have a problem that only you can solve. Everyone else is dead. Hell, I thought you would have joined them by now. But you have this resiliency. You just won't die, and as long as you're taking in air, I have to try and exact information from you. I told you on that first day. You tell me everything you know, you'll see the light again."

Carl understood the power of speech, but he also understood the power of silence. He had made his pitch to Fernando and would give him a moment to consider his options. Once again, he used the bucket to wash away the filth that had amassed around them. Then, he sat back down.

"Are you ready to talk? Or do we need to do this again?"

Every man has his breaking point. A moment where they are willing to broker anything and everything for release. Fernando Suarez had been pushed to the precipice so many times before and pushed back, but he no longer had any will to resist. The aggregate of two years of physical and emotional stress had finally broken his foundation. His body was still recovering from the torment, and he signaled affirmation the only way he had left, by nodding his head up and down.

"I think he's ready," said Abe before pulling out a celebratory cigar.

Carl approached Fernando and popped open another bottle. The sound of it sent a shiver up his spine. But this time there were no pliers. He placed it against Fernando's lips and let him take a sip. It was the first moment of satisfaction he had experienced in ages. Then, finally, after two years, Fernando Suarez spoke.

He could only muster a whisper. Carl leaned forwards and listened as he began to divulge the location of the factory.

"Thank you, Fernando," said Carl, holding out his hand and motioning for Abe. "That's all I ever wanted."

Abe placed a small caliber revolver into Carl's hand.

"I made you a promise," he said, pulling back the hammer of his revolver. "If you told me everything you knew, you would see the light."

Then, he placed the barrel of the gun against Fernando’s temple.

"I'd recommend walking towards it."

CHAPTER TWO

Intelligence work requires a certain level of finesse. The goal for aspiring operatives is to achieve a delicate balance between knowing when to extend a hand and knowing when to throw a punch. Those who excel in this field are the ones who understand that violence can be an immediate solution, but often has unforeseen consequences. Dead men don't talk. Murder turns men into martyrs. It inspires others to take up arms and fight for a cause. Even the most callous, soulless husk of a human being can inspire others to take revenge.

Career men in the agency were the ones who resorted to violence as a worst case scenario. Only reserved for those who could not be bought or bargained with. Power and respect came from navigating these difficult waters. Live by the sword, die by the sword as they say. Never be afraid to wrap your hand around the hilt, but only draw it when you were prepared to strike. Those were the rules that kept agents alive in the field. All of those concepts were meaningless in Colombia.

The war on drugs started with the kind of political haranguing one would expect to find at a peace conference or the United Nations. Rational men sitting across a table from one another trying to logically wrap their head around a complex issue. Using their vast and numerous resources to try and find an amicable plan that would stem the flow of product from South America into the United States. On paper, it seemed like such an attainable goal. First, economic efforts were made to bolster the Colombian military. Train their own people to combat the problem. Send down American assets to educate them. Create an intelligence infrastructure to help identify suspects and bring them to justice. Applying First World techniques to a Third World problem.

The gains were small. For every cartel member brought down, ten more were ready to step in to take their place. And a criminally small percentage made it to trial. Most were murdered in jail either by fellow inmates or corrupt policemen who would make more in ten seconds executing a criminal than they would an entire year of patrolling the streets. If by some small miracle they ever made it to court, the proceeding judges would either be bribed or killed. The cartel's methodology was savage. The drug trade had given them enough to finance a bloody war of retribution against anyone trying to hurt their business. And even small disruptions in the supply had not diminished the demand.

It was the kind of scenario the word quagmire had been created to describe. An insatiable addicted public desperate for product and a cash flush, flourishing industry that would do anything to protect their interests. Eighteen months later, it was decided that civilized methods would no longer work. With the pleasantries having been dispensed with, the cartels and the CIA quietly declared war on one another. They would fight savages with savagery. If they could not control, buy, or bring them to justice, they would employ a scorched earth campaign.

Political oversight would not allow for an all out assault, however there were still ways to wage a war without putting numerous boots on the ground.

The earliest campaigns were based on a concept of escalation. If the cartels killed a witness, the CIA would gun down their dealers in public. A car bomb outside police headquarters would be met with a guided missile into one of their compounds. It was a war fought in the shadows being waged by men with no consideration for collateral damage.

The current campaign was brutally efficient. Find the location of cocaine producing facilities and eviscerate them. Even a group as ruthless as the cartels could not keep everyone silent. The most loyal employee would be hard-pressed to turn down six figures for doing nothing more than pointing to a location on the map.

Carl and Abe had spent the last three years in Colombia. In that time, they had successfully located and destroyed a dozen facilities. Each mission had the same cadence. Military recon would verify the location. A team of trained operatives would penetrate the perimeter and plant high grade explosives which would be detonated in broad daylight, without warning. The vast majority of the hourly wageworkers inside would be killed. Those who survived were dragged out and shot. There were few high value targets. These were manual laborers. Factory workers. People who barely understood the complexities of the politics that required their execution. Calling them pawns felt disingenuous. At least pawns were afforded the dignity to die fighting.

Abe and Carl sat on the hill overlooking the carnage. The latest facility had been hidden underground, managing to avoid air surveillance for the past two years. Explosives were dropped into circulation vents on the surface. The bombs destroyed the interior, and the oxygen starved flames poured out of the vents, erupting the exterior into a fountain of fire. In the aftermath of the blast, the cooked cocaine caught the wind and filtered through the air like fresh, powdery snow.

There was a certain pointlessness to the search for survivors, but Abe believed in being thorough. Both he and Carl smoked a celebratory cigar, yet only Carl looked like he had an interest in celebrating.

"Clever. Very clever," said Carl, his cigar clenched between his teeth.

"Not clever enough," replied Abe scanning the row of bodies strewn across the open field.

"We need to find the other ones fast. Now we know what to look for. And once word gets out, they'll start shuttering the other facilities."

Abe couldn't find the words. The brutality of the scene unfolding before him had absorbed all his attention.

"You all right?" asked Carl.

"Is this what you wanted?" asked Abe, his eyes fixed upon a smoking carcass.

"Absolutely. I'd been wondering how they were getting product produced and transported in the area. Subterranean producing facility and tunnels. Can you imagine how long it took to get this place set up?"

"That's not what I meant, and you know it," replied Abe.

"I know. I was hoping to avoid another one of these philosophical debates you've become so fond of."

"Fuck off."

"Everybody goes through this, Abe. It's perfectly natural. This is difficult work. We're grinding out here one factory at a time. But it's making a difference."

"Do you really believe that?"

"Of course I do. How could I look at something so blissfully tragic and not believe that there's a point?"

"You think we're making a damn bit of difference?" scoffed Abe.

"With what?"

"With stopping the drug trade?"

"The drug trade?" replied Carl, erupting into laughter. "Of course not."

"Then what's the benefit?"

"The benefit is to my career, motherfucker. Do you know how lucky we are to be here, Abe? Do you think they're doing shit like this in Europe or Asia? Fourteen units of soldiers at our command. Engaging an enemy on their home soil. Complete autonomy in our actions. They haven't said no to a single acquired target. I want something reduced to rubble, they ask me 'where and when'. 'Why' doesn't even enter into the equation. They don't even care. How does that not put lead in your pencil?"

Abe had become accustomed to Carl's penchant for grand speeches.

"This is the fucking dream assignment, Abe. War in an age where we don't fight wars anymore. Out there it's all a high tech chess game. High yield, low risk. Painting targets with lasers and waiting for a missile to be fired a thousand miles away. It's a fucking video game out there, Abe. But here... here we get to fight like people were meant to. Eye to eye. Face to face. Staring down your opponent and waiting to throw the haymaker."

Of the many tricks Abe had picked up in South America, tuning out Carl was the most consistently useful. As Carl's grandstanding became little more than pops and clicks in the background, another sound began to cut through the clutter. Down below, one of the soldiers was dragging a young woman through the field. She kicked with what little energy she had, crying the same phrase over and over again.

"La boveda..." she whimpered. "La boveda de Palobar."

It was so low and so random that he might have missed it. Abe stood from his perch and listened again to make sure he heard her correctly.

"Quiet," snapped Abe, cutting Carl off mid-rant.

"What is it?" he replied, following Abe's eye-line to the girl being dragged towards the gutter where the corpses were being piled.

"La boveda de Palobar," she said again.

"What's she saying?" asked Carl.

"Palobar's vault," Abe replied.

"What does that mean?"

Abe descended the hill, not offering any explanation, moving with some expediency. The soldier had dragged her as far as he was willing to carry her, not caring for the resistance. A dead body would be far easier to dispose of. He placed his rifle against the back of her head and prepared to finish the job. She barely had the strength to sit up, her limp body collapsing to the ground.

"Stop," yelled Abe across the field. "Dejar esta

vida!"

Abe lifted her head from the ground and grabbed a canteen from the soldier, pouring water over her lips. She continued to repeat the phrase, adding additional words with each breath.

"La bóveda de Palobar...." she said between sips. "Mi vida por la ubicación de la bóveda de Palobar,"

"I need you to take this woman back to the compound," said Abe, taking off his jacket and wrapping it around her. "Clean her up, get her fed, and make sure no one talks to her but me."

"What the hell, Abe?" said Carl, finally catching up. "This was a zero-sum assignment. If you're hard up for some local tail I know a few places we could go where the women are a little less... scorched..."

"She has information," replied Abe, watching the girl being carried to a Jeep.

"So we're torturing women now? I thought you had a thing about that."

"We're not going to torture her. She offered up information in exchange for her life."

"What kind of information?"

"La boveda de Palobar," said Abe. "Palobar's vault."

CHAPTER 3

Raul Palobar was a charming opportunist and proficient murderer. He lacked the kind of moral compass one needed to succeed in his line of work. For the better part of eight years, he ran the drug trade in Colombia. Like most made men he worked his way from the ground up making alliances and quickly dispatching of the competition. Raul wasn't a despot or an aspiring dictator, merely a passionate believer in unbridled capitalism. A fan of human nature with a simple philosophy that everyone could be bought, bullied, or butchered and was willing to employ any of these techniques to attain his goals.

He brought structure and order to a trade that had never known either. Production doubled, then doubled again. The flow of traffic went from a steady drip to a pour. It had flooded the United States so quickly that it made it nearly impossible for them to engineer a response. Raul was setting up legitimate businesses to launder revenue 18 months before the U.S. Government even knew his name. By the time their investigations had uncovered his identity, he had already dug 60 miles worth of tunnels beneath the Mexican border to funnel his product.

Raul Palobar's sins were many and frequently repeated. His greed was insatiable. In seven years, he had made enough money for a thousand lifetimes, but it was never enough. Gluttony was a constant vice. Lavish mansions, tricked out luxury cars, garish jewelry... he would have it all. It went beyond the normal trappings of money and power. He had spent a hefty sum on a bunker-like facility complete with tennis courts, six Olympic-sized swimming pools, and a fully functional zoo to keep his children entertained. He had perfected gluttony but the sin he found most fulfilling was wrath. It was his medium, and he had spent a decade painting the streets of Columbia blood-red. Raul was vicious in an inhumane way. Like a caged animal that suddenly rediscovers instinct and mauls its captors. Ultimately it wouldn't be greed, gluttony, or wrath that resulted in his downfall, but pride.

Organizing and forcefully merging the cartels may have been good for his bank account, but it gave the U.S. Government something it sorely needed: a single target. Before Raul's ascension into power, the drug trade was a collection of small-time thugs and bandits too busy warring with one another to turn their small operations into the multi-billion dollar monster it had become. Now, there was a linen clad, bejeweled mastermind begging to be dethroned. The head of the snake that could be severed and hoisted onto the world stage for all to see. Raul Palobar believed himself to be untouchable. But every man can be reached. The CIA used his own tactics against him. Raul would not be bullied, and thanks to an obsessive paranoid routine, he could not be butchered. And while there was no sum large enough to buy him out, the same could not be said of his lieutenants, some of whom were eager to take over. Others had become disenfranchised with Raul's opulent ways. A combination of financial remuneration, guaranteed protection, and state sanctioned approval limits of supply coming across the border gave them both the confidence and the wherewithal to end Palobar.

On a sunny fall day while exiting through the rear of a restaurant, Raul Palobar was shot dead. His lifeless body was then extensively photographed before being discarded on the side of the road in a pile of garbage. His execution sent a powerful message to those defiant souls who believed themselves to be untouchable.

Raul was a strong presence. In his absence, a vacuum formed. Those who had brokered deals in exchange for his murder quickly turned on one another. The resulting power struggle fractured the operation which reverted the drug trade to an archaic state in record time. The Government seized his holdings, auctioning off anything of value. Only the husks of his reign remained. Most of his real estate was so far removed from the civilized world that they were cleared out, stripped down to the barest of resources, and abandoned. Not even taking the time to board up windows, leaving them exposed to the elements. In these harsh environments and without maintenance or upkeep they quickly deteriorated. Weathered monuments to avarice.

"La boveda de Palobar?" said Abe, watching her as she sipped soup from a cup.

Her eyes darted up, looking past the rim to her captors. She continued to sip from the cup as she nodded in agreement.

"Dime lo que sabes de él."

"What are you asking her?" said Carl, pouring himself a cup of coffee.

"How the hell did you get this assignment without

speaking Spanish?"

"I know it, I'm just a little rusty."

"I asked her to tell me about the vault."

"She's not talking," said Carl, locking eyes with her. "Maybe she's full of shit."

"Maybe," replied Abe. "Mi amigo piensa que es un farol."

She put down the cup and wiped her lips with her sleeve.

"You're not gonna get anything good from her. Mark my words. Between the shock of the blast and the pain medication you have her pumped up on, she's probably brain-damaged."

"¿Estás bien?" Abe asked.

"That one I know," chimed Carl.

"Congratulations."

She smiled, but still would not speak.

"She's playing you, Abe. Right now, she's surveying the room, putting together an exit strategy. She keeps looking at the syringe tray over there. Probably wants to put a needle into your eye socket and push it through the back of your head."

"No quiero que esto se ponga feo," said Abe. "Pero entiendo que es una opción"

"What'd you tell her?" whispered Abe.

"I told her you were a very small, very angry man with a small penis who overcompensates for his shortcomings by abusing farm animals."

"Not cool."

Her laughter was the first honest reaction she'd had since being cuffed to the chair.

"He said that if I didn't talk, things would get ugly," she said. Her command of the English language was strong.

"She speaks English?" said Carl, who was the only person in the room surprised by this.

"You knew?" she asked Abe.

"More like an educated guess," he replied, offering her a cigarette.

"And he was right," she said, sliding the cigarette slowly and seductively out of the pack before placing it between her puckered lips

"First time for everything," replied Abe.

"Right about what?" asked Carl, still one step behind the rest of the conversation.

"I was trying to figure out how to get out of here. But I wouldn't have put that syringe in your eye. I would have gone for the vein in the neck."

"I like her," said Carl, moving past Abe to offer her a light.

"Of course you do. She wants you dead."

"All of my ex-wives have that in common."

"So the vault," said Abe, trying to get the conversation back on course. "Was that on the level or..."

"It was. Completely on the level," replied Magdalena.

"Tell me about it."

"You already know what it is?" she asked.

"Yes I do. But I don't know that *you* know what it is."

"It's where Palobar supposedly hid his money."

"Everybody knows that part. Every street urchin in Bogotá can tell you about Palobar's vault and how he secretly escaped the death squads and hid his fortune away never to be found," said Abe, circling back around to the girl, flipping back his jacket to reveal a series of knives sheathed in his belt.

"Why don't you stop with the runaround and tell me something I don't know before this becomes less civilized."

"The man who burned and buried a hundred men and women wants to talk about civility?" she said, her disdain readily apparent.

"What was the headcount back there, Carl?" asked Abe, looking to shift the conversation.

"One hundred and six," replied Carl.

"Every civilization requires a foundation. Most often it's built on the backs and bones of those on the losing side. We could sit here and talk philosophy all day. But the only thing that matters is that you're in that chair looking to make a deal. I'm sorry about your one hundred and six friends back there. They are unfortunate casualties in a conflict that I doubt they fully understood. I don't doubt most of them were hard-working, well-intentioned people just looking to make a buck. I don't take any pleasure in putting them in the ground. But trust me when I say this: if you're just biding your time, and you have no card to play here, I could easily make it one hundred and seven."

The severity and shift in tone were subtle, but enough to make her a believer.

"Can I have another cigarette?" she asked.

"Sure," he replied, producing a pack from his coat pocket.

She took the first drag and inhaled deeply, and as she exhaled, she began to tell her story.

"In 1945, at the end of the Second World War, a number of high ranking Nazi officers made their way to South America, shuttled across the Atlantic buying themselves new lives with stolen money and property. Brokering their freedom by paying off Governments with everything from gold to stolen works of priceless art."

"Again, you're not telling me anything I don't already know."

"You're impatient," she replied.

"And temperamental," added Carl from the periphery. "He's also a sore loser."

"I don't need a history lesson," said Abe, lighting up a cigarette. "I need information."

"Come on," barked Carl. "This was just getting good. You want her to skip over the part about Nazi conspirators and backdoor political dealings. Please, my dear, continue."

"When Palobar came into power, he started collecting these assets. The gold bars, the artwork. Laundering hundreds of millions of dollars in cash for items that would be easier to travel with. Things he could use to broker his own freedom should the need arise."

"Ironic," said Abe.

"Not ironic," she said with a hint of venom. "Just interesting."

"So Palobar starts trading sums of cash for gold and classic art. So what happened to it? It couldn't have just disappeared."

"It didn't disappear. It's right where he left it."

"And where would that be?" asked Abe, steadily losing patience.

"In his coastal estate, a bunker he built in the middle of nowhere."

"No way," exclaimed Carl. "They went over that place with a fine toothed comb. Top to bottom. Every rock turned over."

"You're sure about that?"

"Pretty damn sure," replied Abe. "I saw the reports which included X-rays of every wall of the building and radar of every crevice on the grounds. Everything in there that could be found was found."

"Because a man like Palobar wouldn't have considered any of that," she said, directly attacking their ego.

"So where did he hide it?" asked Carl.

"She already told us," replied Abe. "Clever."

"What am I missing?" asked Carl.

"Everything," replied the girl, taking another drag of the cigarette.

"The Nazis, 1945. The ones that were shuttled across the Atlantic," said Abe.

"What about them?" Carl said, struggling to get caught up on the conversation.

"What do you think they were shuttled in?"

"Ok, how about we can the cryptic riddles and just fill me in already."

"It seems the late Mr. Palobar had acquired a submarine," said Abe.

She smiled at Abe. The fact that he had been smart enough to put it together was something of a turn on.

"And if it's still there..." he added.

"It's still there," she said with unrelenting confidence.

"And why are you sharing this with us? Why now?" asked Carl.

"Because as resourceful as she is, she lacks the wherewithal to pull something off of this size," replied Abe, answering for her. "You'd need a trained team, specialized equipment, and deep pockets."

"And even if I could recover it all, what then?" she said, completing the thought. "What good are gold bars and priceless paintings to someone who lacks the means to move them?"

"So you hold onto the information, wait until you can find someone with the means..."

"And then you play the card," she said.

There was a rhythm to their back and forth. Both she and Abe were products of a rough upbringing and had managed to survive because they were smarter. In truth, they were not all that different: survivors who were always planning their next move.

"What's your name?" asked Abe, producing another cigarette.

"Magdalena," she replied, exhaling an acrid cloud of smoke.

"Well Magdalena, I think you and I have a deal to discuss."

CHAPTER FOUR

Magdalena Estevez was a dreamer whose every thought centered on escape. Escaping the poverty of the ghetto where she was born. Escaping the abusive father who tormented her family. Finding a way out of her oppressive country of origin where opportunities for smart young women were limited to service industries. She watched so many of her friends take a similar path, starting as bartenders or servers in a watering hole, eventually talked into prostitution as the only avenue for making any real money. Those who couldn't stomach the sex trade found work for the cartels in processing facilities or making deliveries. This was no career path for someone with Magdalena's aspirations. She wanted a better life than her environment was capable of providing.

There were no women for her to idolize. Not in this squalor where the best an honest woman could hope for was to find a husband and raise a family. Unable to find a female role model, her attention shifted to the men of her corner of the world. The ones who had no trouble crawling their way out of the gutter into positions of power. If they wanted something, they simply took it. One day they were young corner scrappers and thugs working for the cartels, unabated by a depressingly low life expectancy. Those who managed to survive and displayed any modicum of intelligence could work their way up the ranks. All that was required to succeed was the will to commit unspeakable acts and a fearlessness that rendered consequences as a hindrance.

It was easy for her to admire someone like Fernando Palobar. Like her, he had grown up in a poor ghetto with few prospects. He started well below rock bottom and had ascended to the throne. It didn't matter that it required fear, violence, and unspeakable acts to get to that point. She had spent her childhood witnessing countless tragedies and had become all too familiar with suffering. If others were made to suffer in order for her to improve her station in life, so be it. Her fascination with Palobar started out strictly academic but eventually became an obsession. She idolized him like the throngs of teenage girls camped outside a hotel waiting to meet a pop singer.

She hatched a plan to move to Bogotá and find work within his organization. From there, she would find a way to catch his attention. Volunteer for any detail. Taking the most dangerous work. Eventually she would catch his eye. He would recognize her initiative and find a place for her within his inner circle. It was the kind of fevered dream that exists in the troubled minds of the delusional. The reality of the situation was far more sobering. She found entry level work at a processing facility. The same kind of pathetic grind that she had fought to escape in her hometown. But here, it wasn't just a way to make an income. It was a gateway that would lead her to a better life.

The cartel wars put a damper on her plans. The infighting and violence had made her job exceedingly dangerous and the constant threat of reciprocity had forced the families to close ranks. There was little room for career progression. New faces were potential liabilities. The only benefit came from the high body count which allowed Magdalena to work her way from the processing floor into administration. She was now tasked with recruiting laborers for the factory floor. This put her in regular communication with the middle men who kept the gears moving, but it was hardly the fast track to success she had been hoping for.

She spent nearly two years working in talent acquisition, making a name for herself as a smart and savvy employee capable of working independently. She had gained the trust of her employers and was starting to get the kind of compensation that could provide all the things she was denied as a child. In that time, Palobar had evolved from a man of envy to the single most powerful man in Colombia. She began to spend her spare time tracking him whenever he came into the city. Shadowing his movements, finding what establishments he frequented. Becoming familiar with his security detail. Palobar often had multiple caravans throughout the city in a constant state of motion, keeping his enemies unsure of his whereabouts. It took Magdalena only a few weeks to figure out the patterns, and to identify which security guards were the ones trusted with his care.

In a simple spiral notebook, she had managed to crack the code of Palobar's travel pattern and discovered a restaurant he frequented in the south of the city. That was where she would force an introduction, a spontaneous flirtation that would get his attention. From that one conversation he would see the spark that flickered from behind her hazel eyes. He would recognize the drive within her to succeed. He would pluck her from obscurity. Finally her dreams would be realized.

Jabali was a no frills diner known for a modest selection of local delicacies. Traditional Colombian dishes with a cook and owner well trusted by Palobar and his associates. It was a place they could do business and speak freely. Based on Magdalena's calculations, Palobar and his crew would arrive for a meeting the third Thursday of the month. She spent a week's pay preparing for that day. Salons and boutiques to put a fine shine on every inch of her. She would be the most polished thing in Jabali, a shimmering sparkle that stood out against the plaster and tile.

Her heart skipped a beat when he walked through the door, flanked by six men who worked their way to the back of the restaurant. He immediately noticed her. How could he not? She was a vision radiating from the corner of the bar, a far cry from the local girls who frequented the place. Their eyes met as he lowered the thick black Ray-Bans that he rarely removed. They exchanged smiles and a friendly nod before Palobar and company went to their roped off tables at the back of the restaurant. She tried not to be inconspicuous, but it was nearly impossible. Her eyes subconsciously darted towards him every few moments. There he was, in the restaurant with her just a few tables away. If it was going to happen, it had to be today. She knew she couldn't make the first move. Such an obvious gesture would be a dead giveaway. The move had to be his. All she could do was sit and wait, casually picking at the plate of food in front of her.

An hour had passed. The conversation at the back of the room had quieted. A spirited discussion soon turned to more casual laughter as several rounds of drinks were doing a good job of loosening them up. Magdalena began to wonder if her plan would work. That question was answered by the sound of a shot glass being placed on the bar in front of her.

"From the gentleman in the corner," said the bartender.

She looked over, and there he was. Raul Palobar, holding a shot glass high into the air in her honor. She picked up the glass and smiled, throwing it immediately back, then pushing the lime and salt chaser back towards the bartender. Palobar grinned before taking his own shot, then whispered into the ear of an associate. Within moments, he was at the bar asking Magdalena if she would agree to a meeting. From there she was escorted into a bathroom and stripped down in a thorough security check. Merely another indignity she would suffer to make her dreams a reality.

Everything moved in half time as they walked her to the table. There he sat, Raul Palobar, grinning from ear to ear. The others moved away from the table, one remaining security guard pulling out a chair for her to sit.

"My dear," he said, taking her hand in his. "I've been to this restaurant a dozen times, and I don't ever recall seeing anything as fetching. I must know your name."

"Magdalena," she replied, trying not to let her welling emotions overcome her.

"What brings you here, and don't insult me by

telling me the lomo al trapo."

"I'm not sure I know what you mean."

"Of course you do," he said while lighting a cigarette. "You wanted to catch my eye. You caught it. Now what do you want to do with it?"

He had no time for games, nor was he interested in the dance. He was a man of business. It was one of the things that most attracted her to him.

"I actually work for you," she said.

"Everybody works for me," he replied. "What do you do?"

"I work in Chapinero, screening labor."

"Do you like it?" he asked.

"It's a good job."

"No. It's a shit job," he said, signaling for another round of drinks. "I used to do it. There's no reliability at that level. Everyone's looking to take a little off the top."

"Trust is always an issue," she said, trying to remain active in the conversation.

"Trust is at the heart of everything in this business. Without it, you have nothing."

His voice made her tremble. There was gravity to every word he uttered.

"So can I trust you, Magdalena?" he asked.

"Of course, Mr. Palobar."

"Please. Call me Raul."

"All right... Raul," she replied with a smile.

They spoke for another twenty minutes before retreating to the men's room. The conversation wasn't nearly as productive as she'd hoped. There were nerves, and the constant concern that if she came on too strong he would retreat. Every man says they want a strong woman, but the truth is men of power are more interested in compliance than confidence. There, in the limited privacy of the bathroom, Magdalena shared an intimate moment with the man she had idolized for so many years as he manhandled her atop the sink. It was hardly the fruition of all her fantasies, but it was enough.

"Call Antoine Delgado," he said as he zipped up, producing a business card from his pocket. "I think we could use someone with your talents in somewhere other than the factory."

He gave her one last glance before exiting the bathroom. Once he was gone, she allowed herself to shed some joyful tears. So many people dream. So few possess the wherewithal to make them a reality. Magdalena Estévez had met her idol, and now had an opportunity to move up into his organization.

She was ten feet out the front door when she heard the shot. Curiosity sent her into the alley towards the back of the restaurant. From the corner she could see him on the ground, the crimson blood pouring from his coughing mouth. Two more shots to the head ceased all movement, and before she could even process the tragedy unfolding before her, four men in suits threw his lifeless body into the back of a van leaving the corpses of his security detail strewn about.

His death did not sate her obsession for Palobar. If anything, it compounded her interest. She had spent so much time learning about him, tracking his movements, cataloging his behaviors. After he passed, she continued to cobble together information, managing to work her way into his funeral services and was clever enough to finagle a copy of the file kept on him by the Colombian Police. She pored over every detail with the kind of magnifying glass reserved for profilers and biographers. When his fortune went missing, she was one of the few smart enough to connect the dots and fill in the gaps. The sad reality was that Magdalena knew Fernando Palobar almost as well as anyone on this Earth.

As the legend of his vault grew from whispered story to urban legend, she was the only one with the dedication to try and finish his story. The world's most notorious drug lord had been killed, and not a penny of his fortune had been recovered. Palobar had died, and to many he was nothing more than a cautionary tale. To Magdalena, the vault was his legacy. Finding it and proving its existence became her new obsession.

Eventually, she had to return to work finding the only job she had ever excelled at: talent acquisition, taking a position with one of the many splinter factions that carved up Palobar's kingdom. Patience was her strong suit. She would wait, earn enough money to mount a pilgrimage to Vaina de la Laga and one day prove her theory correct. No matter the dramatic turns her life had taken she still dreamed, every thought still centered on escape.

CHAPTER FIVE

Nightfall had brought some respite. The heat had become more bearable, but the humidity still made the air heavy. Everything in this climate was covered in a layer of sweat. On the books, recovering Palobar's vault could be a feather in their cap. Off the books, it could be their golden parachute. There were strong arguments against bringing this information to their superiors. It could be nothing more than a ruse. The ramblings of a crazy woman trying to save her own skin. Wasting valuable resources and manpower on a weak lead certainly wouldn't reap any benefits. There was still a chance that this was nothing more than a wild goose chase. They would go through the paces and discuss all of these carefully constructed and valid points, at least to give the appearance of considering doing this above board. But there was no chance of that happening. This was the kind of haul that would make even the most rigid company man break ranks.

"It's big," said Carl.

"Enormous," replied Abe, wiping away the sweat on his head with a kerchief.

"Let's say she's not lying."

"She's not lying."

"We get down there, we find this thing. It's loaded with gold, and art… then what?"

"It's a submarine."

"That's not an answer."

"We pilot it out and take it north."

"That would be a great plan, if either of us knew how to pilot a fifty-year-old submarine."

"So we'll need to find one."

"That's four," said Abe holding up four fingers.

"We'll need at least a six man team to get us there."

"That's eight."

"You're counting us?" asked Carl with a smile on his face. "I don't know about you, I'm a little rusty on the basic training."

"You'll do fine."

"If they're tied to a chair, I'm your guy. Actual tactical combat might be another story."

"Every warm body we bring is another warm body we have to pay… or silence."

"No point in taking this on if we're not going to do it right."

"Fine," said Abe, rubbing his forehead. "Who do we need first?"

"We're going to need someone who knows the lay of the land."

CHAPTER SIX

Neal Barstow had left the comforts of the First World behind after receiving his draft card. He was a trained hunter and had a savage streak that he fought hard to keep below the surface. There were primal urges in him that he spent his entire childhood masking. The urge to hurt animals and inflict violence on those who mocked him. Like many adolescent victims, Neal was small for his age, hitting his growth spurt far later than his peers. Once he did finally begin to grow, the proportions were a bit off, transitioning him from a small boy to a thin, wiry framed man. It was around middle school that they began to call him 'Nil' as an estimate of his worth. Eventually he would adopt the moniker in an attempt to take away the power it held over him.

He poured his angst into the outdoors, becoming proficient in a number of weapons as well as mastering the art of survival. Nil would have made an ideal soldier. His ferocity was matched only by his intelligence. Not book smart, mind you, but the kind of predatory understanding of human nature. Nil had spent his whole life silently studying those around him and a near photographic memory allowed him to create a kind of social index which gave him the uncanny ability to predict behaviors and catch lies. While the Army may have had big plans for Nil, he had his own. With no interest in fighting for a society he found to be perverse, Nil headed south across the Mexican border, making his way on a 10-year journey through Central America. He lived off the land, occasionally emerging to work odd jobs for a span of a few months when he required supplies. Driver, fisherman, security detail, hard laborer. No job was beneath him.

His skill set brought him to the attention of those running the burgeoning drug trade. Nil was a man who knew how to stay off the radar. This was a great asset to a growing number of enterprising entrepreneurs. And with Nil's rusty moral compass, he had no issue doing the kind of gritty grinding required of hired hands. It was while in the employ of a Guatemalan drug cartel that Nil found the one thing his life had been lacking: respect. No longer was he the ignored or picked on child, or the lanky zero. He was appreciated, respected, and somewhat feared. He took pride in this and would spend the rest of his days seeking out this very specific type of validation.

He was twenty-two when he took his first life, quite by accident. A bare fisted boxing match went from a simple competition to a brutal confrontation. Nil had always been a good fighter, but it wasn't until he was beaten half to death that he was able to tap into his reserves, a well of rage and spite that he had swallowed for much of his life. Once unleashed, it was like watching a tortured animal released from imprisonment. Six brutal strikes had fractured his opponent's skull, the bone fragments piercing his brain. He died before he achieved a horizontal state.

It was only a matter of time before someone like Nil made his way to Colombia. Central America was the highway where the trade was trafficked and the product flowed North. But it was South America where the money flowed and where fortunes were made. While Nil had never had much concern for money, his newfound sense of pride compelled him to find a more worthy group of peers for his talents to be employed.

It took little time for him to find work where the emerging cartels made use of his skills. Much of his value to the organization came from his identity. Xenophobic Americans were more comfortable doing business with their own. The melting pot was a fine philosophy, but it did little to bridge trust between enterprising Americans setting up a distribution network and their cartel suppliers. Nil became that bridge acting as a liaison and helped construct a comprehensive pipeline of product and cash that pleased both parties.

Nil had finally achieved the respect he had searched for, though he found little satisfaction in the political aspects of this role. He was a man of action, someone who relished getting his hands dirty. And while there were precious few in this burgeoning industry who could describe themselves as clean, he found himself pining to return to a more active role in the business. The cartel wars would provide him such an option.

Palobar's ascension into power was hardly bloodless. As the money poured in, the cartels would argue over proper royalties while the ruling families started to become creative with the accounting. Trust was a sorely lacking commodity in this trade. A handful of small skirmishes soon escalated into an all out war. Each family circled the wagons and entered an eighteen-month conflict that produced a body count that rivaled several small 20th century wars.

It was Palobar who emerged victorious. An unlikely winner in a conflict whose brutality and ruthlessness saw few rivals. His family had the smallest piece of the business, but he was willing to fight the hardest to maintain their share. Charisma, intimidation, and fear bought him many allies. Strategy and business acumen put him in the right place to assume control as the families slaughtered one another. Palobar was the firm hand that was needed to hold everything together. Nil had made a name for himself during the war as a brutal enforcer for the Dias family who mercilessly slaughtered those who would oppose them. Most notably for a Christmastime incident involving nine decapitated heads delivered in meticulously wrapped present boxes.

Eventually the cartel wars ended, not on the battlefield or the streets of Bogota but at a boardroom table. A new order was negotiated and hostilities ended with signatures and witnesses. It was hardly the big finish Nil was hoping for. In his mind, the cartel wars would end with him standing over the dead body of Fernando Palobar as he watched him take his final breath, crimson blood pouring from his slit throat. Sadly, that would never happen.

From there, Nil's employment prospects quickly dried up. Palobar would never allow anyone who worked for the Dias family to climb into any role of authority. On top of that, Palobar also had an immense distrust of Americans within his organization. To him, they were potential risks likely to be used by the CIA to get a foothold into his operations.

Over the next two years everything Nil had built had been lost. He tried to set up his own small operation, investing heavily in producing and distributing small quantities, but lacked the skills to oversee all aspects of the operation. The investment cost him dearly. He squandered the rest of his money on gambling and liquor. He considered returning to the highways of the trade he had helped engineer, but his reputation was tarnished beyond redemption. The cartel wars had elevated his profile too high, preventing him from finding even entry level work. Nil then retreated back into the shadows, far from the beaten path. Though he could no longer participate in the trade, he was still a knowledgeable asset with nearly two decades of experience about the region and the personalities that held power there. For the right price, he would be willing to share.

In person, Nil didn't seem to match the brutal persona that had become attached to him, save for an eye patch over his left eye. His office was a corner booth at a seedy bar in Popayán. With his long arms outstretched, his one good eye sunken in, and a single light cast down from above on his sallow skin made him look more like the carcass of Neal Barstow. A man reduced to nothing. Truly he had lived up to his moniker.

"A submarine pilot?" asked Nil, taking a drag from his cigarette. "That's gonna cost you."

"Let's just assume for the sake of argument that's not a problem," said Abe, sticking out like a sore thumb in his sports coat and dress shirt.

"I know a guy. He's old. If the pistons are still firing, he can get you where you need to go."

"Great," said Abe. "How do we get the ball

rolling on this?"

"First, I'm going to need to know why."

"The why is irrelevant," said Carl, equally glaring in a linen ensemble that would be better suited for the deck of a yacht than this grimy rock they were currently crawling under. "We don't need him to know why, we just need him to drive."

"The 'why' is not for him. It's for me," replied Nil, signaling for another round of drinks. "Call it intellectual curiosity."

"An educated man would understand that knowledge is dangerous," said Abe examining the curious smudges on the half clean glass of tequila. "The 'why' creates a loose end. One that eventually needs tying up."

"Look boys. I can appreciate your commitment to keeping ranks, but the truth is you need me a hell of a lot more than I need you. If you can pull this off without someone to drive your submarine, then there's the door. If you can't, put your cards on the table and loop me in."

Both Abe and Carl had been doing this long enough to conceal their tells. They looked straight ahead maintaining their posture and eye line. Both were well aware of the accuracy of his statement, but every negotiation requires that moment where you have to decide whether to forge ahead or walk away. In those instances, Abe took the lead.

"We have intel on a submerged submarine that may contain some assets we need to recover."

"Assets," said Nil with a smile. "What kind?"

"That's classified," said Carl.

"Classified to whom?" replied Nil. "Are you going to sit there and tell me this in an agency operation? The fact that you're sitting on the other side of this table tells me a whole other story. So let's try this again. What kind of assets?"

"The kind that will allow us to handsomely pay whoever helps us recover them."

Once again, the table went silent as both parties considered their next move.

"Fine. You don't want to tell me what. How about where?"

"Northeast of Barranquilla," said Carl.

"Northeast of Barranquilla?" repeated Nil as the cylinders began to turn. "Why there's nothing up there but..."

Click.

The negotiation game ended as a flood of emotion began to pump through Nil's veins so strong you could almost see it through his paper thin skin. There would be no more calculated moves.

"Palobar," he said as the secondhand smoke exited through his nose like two industrial smokestacks. "You're going to Vaina de la Laga?"

Neither answered. They didn't need to. He had put it all together.

"I'll get you your pilot," said Nil, snuffing out the remainder of his cigarillo.

"Your normal fee?" asked Carl, reaching into his coat pocket.

"No," replied Nil. "If you want my help on this, I'm coming with you."

"Give me one good reason why I should entertain that level of crazy," said Abe incredulously.

"Because this deal ain't happening without my involvement."

Abe reached into his pocket, pulled out some

money and placed it on the table before standing up.

"Mr. Barstow, we appreciate your time, but I don't think we will be able to do business together on this particular venture."

"Wait," said Nil, showing his desperation. "You need me."

"No operation is contingent on one person. We can make other arrangements."

"I can be valuable. You'll need a guide."

"We can find another guide," said Carl as they made their way to the door.

"Can you find one that's been there before?" said Nil.

Abe and Carl stopped just short of the door and turned back.

"I can get you your pilot, and I can get you there. How's that for a deal?"

It was an offer too good to refuse.

CHAPTER SEVEN

Jonas Brecht was a broken man. The Great War had taken the lower half of his left leg, but it was his soul that had been fractured beyond repair. He would never get over the losses suffered in that godforsaken conflict. His hopes, his dreams, whatever good had existed in him had been extinguished. Eventually his body healed. With the aid of a wooden prosthetic and cane, he would walk again. But it was through the National Socialist Party that he found his will. It was the cause that got him out of bed every day. The insatiable drive to take back what he had lost. Jonas believed the world was a wicked place in desperate need of purity. He smiled as Germany marched across Europe, and served the leaders of the party with unflinching loyalty. His affliction prevented him from joining the fight and taking up arms, so he would find other ways to be of use.

His background was in education. As a young man he studied mathematics and engineering with the hopes of one day pursuing his doctorate. The First World War had derailed those dreams, but he still possessed a strong analytical mind and an educational background. Eventually he made his way to the naval academy, teaching the basic mechanics of piloting U-Boats to willing cadets. Towards the end of the war, when the end became all but inevitable, Jonas was finally able to step out from behind the podium and take a more active role. The highest ranking members of the party began to put together an exit strategy that required trust and secrecy. Only the most faithful to the party were asked to participate. And so Jonas Brecht was tasked with assembling a bare-bones crew to help chart safe passage for those looking to flee the rapidly deteriorating state.

For the next twelve years, Jonas Brecht navigated the stormy waters of the Atlantic aboard the Kreigsadler, moving the upper echelon of the party to their self-imposed South American exile. Throughout forty voyages, Jonas Brecht's resolve never wavered. The same could not be said of his heart which slowly withered after watching his beloved nation falter a second time. His death was unspectacular, passing in his sleep just a day's journey from his homeland. In spite of his tireless devotion to the party, he was given an unceremonious burial at sea, committed to the waters he had traversed for nearly a decade in service of a nation that no longer had any use for him. A simple entry in the ship's log commemorated the moment:

"Pilot Brecht passed. Discarded body."

The Kreigsadler would continue on for twenty-four more voyages. Jonas Brecht had passed along his trade to a son, Aren, who was just a boy when the war started and was piloting the last remaining German U-Boat by his seventeenth birthday. Aren didn't share his father's passion for the cause, but he respected his wishes enough to continue his work. Like his father, he became a necessary utility. A product of convenience. Unlike his father, he negotiated high fees for his services. He had no loyalty to these men who had used his father for so many years. Aren Brecht learned how to pilot a U-Boat from his father, but he also learned the malignancy of blind devotion to a cause. A mistake he would not repeat.

"How much?" asked Aren, placing a tray of tea and cookies on a coffee table.

"Direct," said Carl, reaching for the sugar. "I like direct."

"I was hoping you'd tell us," said Abe, eying the fine porcelain serving china. "I'd be lying if I told you I had any idea what this kind of job requires."

"It's been awhile," said Aren as he poured himself a cup. "The last time I did this, I was a younger man. How far?"

"How far?" said Carl, unsure of the nature of the question.

"How far am I being asked to pilot this boat of yours?"

"Mexico," said Abe, still staring at the intricate pattern woven into the tea set. Most of his attention was focused on the decor. The entire room seemed out of place in the small Spanish colonial house where Aren Brecht lived. The furniture was European, as was most of the art that adorned the walls. The silver spoons on the tea tray were antiques. These were the trappings and opulent trimmings of a wealthy man, the kind of avarice one wouldn't expect to find in a ramshackle house far off the beaten path.

"Mexico isn't more than a two days journey, barring unforeseen circumstances."

"Unforeseen circumstances like what?" asked Carl.

"Like the United States Navy who have a nasty

habit of monitoring the waters in that region rather heavily. You can thank Mr. Castro for that."

"What do you know about those waters?" asked Abe.

"I know that eight years ago your friend Mr. Palobar had a plan to move cocaine to the United States using submarines. He had a grand plan to create underwater shipping lanes using a fleet of subs he was going to buy from the Soviets. I was asked to consult."

"I'm assuming that didn't go well."

"Mr. Palobar was a man of great vision," said Aren before taking a sip of his tea. "But he was an impatient man who didn't want to deal with the details."

Nil seethed in the background as he rifled through the impressive collection of books that lined the walls. Just hearing the mention of Palobar's name was enough to set him on edge.

"He sent one boat out to sea, and it never came back. The story I heard was that they ventured off course and ended up being sunk just north of Panama."

"That's something we'd like to avoid," said Carl.

"Obviously," replied Aren. "I have no interest in a suicide mission."

"So we're back to the question of cost."

"A one way trip through hostile waters," said Aren as he crunched the numbers in his head. "I expect $80,000 would be fair, and return airfare of course."

"Of course," replied Carl. "Abe?"

Abe was doing his own math, still taking in the many details in the room.

"I believe we can make that work, Mr. Brecht."

"Excellent," replied Aren. "Why don't you let me escort you into town. We can have lunch and discuss the details."

Abe took his last sip of tea, and then turned the cup upside down to find a Nazi swastika etched into the porcelain. The entire room was lined with ill-gotten gains. A time capsule to a bygone era. A tribute constructed by the elder Brecht and left intact by his son out of respect for his father's misguided loyalty.

CHAPTER EIGHT

Christian and Carlos Guittierez were the day laborers of the mercenary world. The kind of hired hands you picked up when you needed something dirty done right. They possessed a variety of skills that proved useful in these lawless corners of existence. Experienced survivalists, proficient in tactical weaponry, capable of working high end construction equipment. They were rarely the least expensive option, but like in all trades, you got what you paid for. Over the years they had picked up the reputation of being unkillable. Hired guns had a life expectancy that could usually be measured in months. An eight year career had helped cement their status as the defacto option when you needed no-questions asked utility work.

Their hiring didn't come without certain peculiarities. There was a hefty amount of ego at play, a product of the Guittierez brothers embracing their indomitable stature. In addition, the brothers had begun to exhibit more theatrics into their work, wearing hand painted tactical masks which were more befitting a comic book or a wrestling ring than the battlefield. Having a knack for survival and a reputation for walking out of a bad situation alive had put them in the catbird seat. They could now pick and choose what jobs they wanted to take. After four years of taking work that could at best be described as 'risky' and at worst 'suicidal', these two poor brothers from the ghettos of Tumaco were making a decent living. Money had never been a priority, but it began to afford them comforts they had never known. Eventually the lure of a higher paycheck became less important than the threat level of the work being performed. There was a rush of adrenaline they craved, a peak level that only came from the most harrowing of life-threatening scenarios.

Addiction comes in many forms. For some it's drugs or alcohol. For others it manifests itself sexually or by engaging in criminal actions. For Christian, it was still a healthy level of exploration. The kind you find in daredevils and stuntmen. Finding ways to put their life on the line, but always with a tether of safety involved. Christian was a thrill seeker, but he had no death wish. Carlos was another story. His work had carved out something sinister in his soul. The only thing that could stir any emotion within him anymore was the surge that ran up and down his spine when his life was in danger. The cold sweats that accompany the fear of taking your final breath.

The spaces between jobs felt almost infinite to Carlos. There was a restlessness within him as he struggled to find any sense of peace when not caught in the crossfire. He had taken to underground cage fighting in the hopes of venting his pent-up aggressions. When that didn't work, he changed to high stakes gambling which he turned out to be quite good at. His poker face was impregnable. On a few occasions, he had even managed to convince others to engage in rounds of Russian Roulette. Staring death in the face was the only thing driving Carlos forward. He relished every opportunity to do so.

Christian Guittierez was dancing with death. His brother Carlos was courting her.

While their penchant for flair clashed with Abe and Carl's more subtle sensibilities, they were smart enough to recognize that the job required muscle. Unlike their most recent acquisitions, there would be no need to haggle or convince Carlos and Christian to take the job. It was only a question of their availability.

CHAPTER NINE

The first leg of the journey was the easiest. A chartered cargo plane would take them to the small town of Tilonegron. During the height of the cartel wars, it was one of many pop-up towns that had been erected, serving as a fuel depot and trading post. A functioning airstrip with a handful of quickly assembled stick frame buildings that had all but fallen apart due to neglect. This would put them 60 miles from the compound. Three days on foot through harsh terrain.

The steady rain poured with no sign of respite. The slate gray clouds loomed overhead, endlessly tumbling from horizon to horizon. The unforgiving weather severely lowered the odds of another human encounter as they navigated through the thick brush, moving ever closer to their destination. But there was more to fear in these woods than other humans. The dense jungle seethed with a number of potential threats. The hard rain masked a number of predators that lurked in the shadows and beneath the bushy brush. There were the snakes that navigated deftly underneath the roots of the largest trees, camouflaged and almost indistinguishable from the browns of the mud and bark.

Nil had spent so many years in this climate that he had become accustomed to scanning the ground and low-lying branches for poisonous serpents. His one good eye darted from space to space, his hands clenched tightly around his rifle. A single bite could be the difference between life and death. Even the anti-venom he carried with him would only delay the inevitable. Being so far removed from civilization, they would never make it to proper medical care in time. There was another predator Nil was more concerned about. Something he caught wind of as they last departed camp. He couldn't shake the feeling that they were being watched, and as they ventured further into the jungle, he began to notice the absence of sound. He could hear no monkeys in the treetops, and the only rustling to be heard was their own. The silence was troubling. It meant the presence of something formidable, something that would have the ability to scare off everything else in the area. Nil was smart enough to keep his suspicions to himself. The last thing they needed at this fragile juncture was panic. However, in his addled mind he was already preparing for the inevitable confrontation.

The terrain proved difficult for Aren. His introverted, low impact life left him ill prepared for the stresses of the jungle. The aching feet, the strain on his lower back, the perpetual sweat that coated every inch of him. This was a level of punishment he wasn't built for.

"We need to stop," said Aren, already discarding his backpack and settling into a sitting position at the base of a tall tree.

"Stopping isn't an option," said Nil, still surveying the surrounding landscape.

"We need to rest," he replied, opening up his canteen. "We should conserve our strength for what's ahead."

"I'm more worried about what's behind us," said Nil, moving away from the group and further into the forest.

Out of habit, Christian and Carlos looked over their shoulders. The thought of being tracked instantly made the group uneasy.

"You think something's following us?" asked Carl, his hand instinctively moving to his service revolver.

"I don't think. I know."

"How many?" asked Abe, already attempting to formulate a plan.

"Just one... far as I can tell."

"One what?" asked Magdalena.

"My guess would be a jaguar. Alpha male, looking to assert a little dominance."

"You're worried about an animal?" asked Abe. "We've got six armed men with enough firepower to level a small town."

"Guns only work if you can see him coming," said Nil who seemed to relish every cryptic thought he uttered.

"I'm sorry," said Aren, taking off his shoes and rubbing his sore feet. "I just need a moment. And if we're incapable of basic human civility and pausing this death march, maybe we should just turn back now."

Abe looked to Carl, both of them realizing the fundamental nature of the problem at hand: Aren held all the cards, being the only one capable of getting the submarine out to sea. Every single member of the party was expendable, except for Aren.

"If we need to rest, we rest," said Abe. "Everybody take five. Nil, Christian, Carlos... do a perimeter sweep. Make sure we're not in any danger."

Abe's choices were hardly random. Friction was a complication that they had neither the time nor the patience for. Conversations would be had.

"How you holding up?" asked Abe, taking a knee next to Aren.

"I've been better," replied Aren. "My knees are giving me trouble. I'm not as spry as I used to be."

"None of us are," said Abe, trying to keep the conversation friendly.

"That savage you have leading us is obsessed. He talks to himself. Have you noticed?"

"I didn't bring him for his conversation skills. I hired him because he knows this territory better than anyone. You might not care for his eccentricities, but he's not here to amuse you: he's here to guarantee your safety."

Meanwhile, Carl handled the other side of the conversation.

"Nil, seriously. You gotta take it easy on him."

"Taking it easy is a luxury we don't have out here," he replied, avoiding eye contact with Carl and continuing to scan the area.

"We need him," said Carl, being as direct as possible. "And we need him not in a perpetual state of panic."

"You don't want him to know what he's getting into?"

"I don't want him shutting down. He's fragile. He's not like us. He's a civilian." Carl paused to let the words sink in. "He's the means to an end, so we might need to do a little coddling."

Nil's expression turned sour. Weakness was

something he had little tolerance for.

"And might I remind you, you brought him into this. This is your guy. So cut him some slack. Not everybody is accustomed to this kind of environment."

Nil thought for a moment. Carl had made his points directly. If nothing else, Nil appreciated the direct approach.

"Fine," he said, shouldering his rifle. "But understand that ignorance is a liability."

"Trust me Nil, if anyone understands that concept, it's me."

They would only cover a few more miles before having to stop. This was not the kind of territory that one could wander blindly through. Flashlights and lanterns were little more than painted targets for anyone else that could potentially be in the area, or the ghostly predators that kept Nil's mind occupied. Fire was a far better option. It provided warmth, as well as light, and in a pinch could be used to ward off any attacker or in a drier season help smoke out potential threats.

There were natural groupings once they had set up camp. Christian and Carlos cleaned their weapons while sharing a flask of whiskey. They laughed and told stories in their native tongue, showing little interest in forming any social alliances within the group. Magdalena stayed close to Abe and Carl, displaying an uneasiness with the rest of the group. Aren hovered close to the fire, the light from the flames illuminating his sunken features. Nil remained perpetually vigilant, sharpening his machete on the outskirts of the small camp.

"You seem on edge, my friend," said Aren to Nil,

addressing his perpetual vigilance.

"Edges keep you sharp," he replied, looking up from the blade with his one good eye.

"You're worried about what? An animal?" he said incredulously.

"It's something more than an animal," he replied, continuing to run the sharpening stone up the length of the blade. "The Quimbayas believed that the jungle cats that inhabited these woods were instruments of vengeance."

Everyone else's conversations stopped as Nil began to spin his tale.

"They used to tell stories of a black jaguar that stalked wayward travelers and only attacked those who weren't pure of heart."

Christian translated for Carlos, who had still not taken the time to learn English.

"Well, then I guess we've got nothing to worry about, right?" said Carl, trying to alleviate the rising tension.

"They called it Obsidiana," said Nil, continuing his ghost story. "Its eyes were as dark as coal. Pitch black. And once you locked eyes with it, you froze. They didn't think it was an animal... they thought it was a ghost."

"Why?" asked Abe.

"Because Obsidiana never fed on its victims. It was after something else... the dark souls of those it hunted."

"A ghost cat?" exclaimed Aren. "Seriously? I suppose next you'll be telling me we need to worry about vampires and werewolves."

Nil looked over to Aren, the deadpan expression slowly turning to a smile. Then a laugh. The others joined in, the laughter contagious, and the entire camp finally had a much needed moment of levity.

"Vampires?" said Nil, wiping a tear away from his eye. "Everybody knows vampires don't travel this close to the equator."

Nil turned his attention back to the blade. The rest of the group sat in a shared awkward silence trying to make sense of a man who had little to spare.

CHAPTER TEN

The unforgiving terrain had finally opened up into a more manageable path. The last remnants of the clearing that had been done to erect Palobar's estate. The brush and thickets made way for tall grass that shifted back and forth like the tides. Magdalena had moved to the front of the group. There was an eagerness and anticipation in every step as she pushed through soreness in her feet. She was half a day's journey from her own private Mecca.

The others had loosened up dramatically, a combination of being beaten down by the elements and growing more comfortable with one another. Carlos and Christian chatted back and forth in their native tongue. Abe reviewed blueprints and maps of the area focused on the cartography. Aren had achieved a manageable level of discomfort. All except Nil who continued to lead with the barrel of his gun. Lowering his guard was never an option.

Something stirred to the south. Nil had been aware of it for days, barely able to catch a hint of its scent as it stayed perpetually downwind to avoid detection. The others had become comfortable with their surroundings. They spoke at a normal volume, unconcerned of giving away their location to predators. Food was being consumed out in the open in spite of multiple warnings. From his point of view, the party had not only stopped respecting this hostile environment, but were brazenly defying the laws of nature. He could no longer guarantee their safety, but was committed to preserving his own.

While the others set up camp, Nil moved to the outer perimeter of the clearing and waited. His back was turned to the campsite pointing into the dark mass of the jungle as the setting sun began to erase every detail of the trees. If death was coming, he intended to stare it down. He wrapped his hand around his revolver, waiting for it to emerge from the black void.

At first, it appeared as nothing more than two shimmering orbs, the moonlight splitting into an infinite number of pinpoints. The heavens circled in the space between its iris and cornea. Then, as it slowly inched from the darkness, the outline of its slender frame became clear.

"Obsidiana," said Nil, frozen by the spinning infinity of its blackened eyes.

His finger quivered as he wrapped it around the trigger, using all his will to pull the rifle up to line up a shot. The beast remained still as Nil lined up the rifle, seemingly oblivious to the danger it posed. At this range it would only take one shot to kill the jaguar, but Nil could not bring himself to pull the trigger.

"Nil!" shouted Carl from the other side of the camp, noticing his raised rifle. "Do you see something?"

He didn't answer, watching as the pitch black jaguar looked past him to the rest of the group. Rather than engaging, the animal turned and descended back into the darkness.

At daybreak, they could see the outline of the estate, each of them convinced a better future awaited just beyond the horizon.

CHAPTER ELEVEN

The exterior of Vaina De La Laga looked as though it had endured a hundred harsh winters and a hundred more dry summers. The stone and marble had lost its luster. The wood had splintered and had been stripped of most of the paint and varnish. A relic of the past no more than ten years old. A sinking foundation had ruined its once pristine architecture, the product of water seeping into the house after the Colombians, the Americans, and the looters had stripped it bare. This was the last surviving monument to Raul Palobar, barely able to stand on its own. A garish spectacle that had once been the most expensive house ever constructed on this continent, now reduced to whatever remnants could not be sold for profit and the timber and stone too heavy to cart away.

Even in its current state, it was a sight for sore eyes as the weary travelers had finally arrived at their destination. Bloodied, but not yet beaten, still elated by the idea that somewhere on this property was a fortune that would forever change their lives.

"We made it," said Aren, immediately discarding his backpack and falling back into a sitting position in the overgrown grass of the front lawn.

"So what now?" asked Nil.

"Now we find the vault," replied Carl, suppressing an epic grin.

"First, we set up a camp," said Abe, moving towards the main house.

"How long do we plan on being here?" asked Magdalena.

"Don't get eager," replied Abe, sticking to his no nonsense approach to everything. "It'll be dark soon. And the mistake we don't want to make is forging ahead without looking where we're stepping first."

"Pragmatic," said Nil. "I respect that."

"Let's get set up in the house. Get a good night's rest. At dawn, we start a hard target search of the property."

There was a flurry of activity around the side of the house. The sound of birds loudly squawking. Further investigation revealed a flock of peacocks moving across the lawn, seemingly unaware of the first human visitors in almost two years. They moved about in a disorderly fashion, zigging left and zagging right, bumping into one another with a lack of regard like a group of inebriated tourists stumbling from a bar.

One of them walked up to the group, stumbling every few steps before bumping into Abe. When it finally stopped, it looked up revealing its blank, expressionless eyes. The peacock blinked for a moment, and then snapped into form, its hind feathers shooting up and letting out a loud, defensive squawk designed to intimidate potential attackers. The others followed suit, first projecting their fear and anger towards the group. Then, in the scrum that had formed, they began to snap at one another.

"What's wrong with them?" asked Magdalena.

"They might not be used to company," said Carl.

They continued to snap and charge at one another for a moment. Then, it stopped without resolution. The peacocks started twitching their heads left and right before continuing their awkward walking pattern away from the house.

The interior of the house provided basic shelter from the elements, however exposure had turned it into a creaking, shifting domicile. The water-soaked wood swelled and retracted. Every floorboard was sunken or splintered and sounded like it was snapping with each step. The wind cut through the holes in the torn roof, producing a low-pitched moan that echoed through every corner of the house. It was as if the house was dying and made its suffering known to any poor soul foolish enough to enter.

There was very little rest achieved. Some were uncomfortable with the surroundings. The sounds, the shifting light and shadows needled the superstitious. Others were restless, either from the anticipation or trepidation of what lay ahead.

Abe dealt with his sleeplessness by falling into familiar patterns. He sat in the old master bedroom with the blueprints sprawled out on the floor in front of him, the room illuminated by a small lantern. There were markings on the architectural renderings, places where he believed access points could exist. He would spend every waking moment memorizing the corridors, familiarizing himself with the exits, and formulating a plan for every stage of the operation. Leave nothing to chance. That was the philosophy that fueled Abe.

The ambient noise masked a number of things in the old plantation house. Under normal circumstances, he might have heard her enter the room instead of three taps she made on the door frame.

"Can I come in?" she asked.

"Of course," he replied, only looking up with his eyes.

She walked around the room slowly, taking in every inch of it. The master bedroom. This is where he slept. This is where he made decisions. This is where he rested after forging his empire.

"Did you ever have any dealings with him?"

"Who?" asked Abe, too focused on what was ahead to be aware of the moment.

"Palobar," she replied.

"Once, years back," he said, circling some points on the photographed overview of the property. "He came to us about the promise of uniting the cartels and needed... funding."

"That sounds like him," she replied with a smile. "Fearless."

"That's one word for it," he replied. His dismissive tone did not sit well with her.

"You didn't care for him?" she asked, taking a seat on the floor.

"To be honest, I never thought much of him. I sure as hell didn't think he was going to pull off as much as he did."

"He surprised people," she replied.

"I suppose he did."

Abe noticed her wandering attention as she looked around the room.

"What about you?"

"What about me?"

"Did you know him? Were you close?"

"I worked for him," she replied. "We shared a few meaningful moments."

She always spoke about him with a hint of romanticism. On a normal day, Abe would have picked up on the subtle social cues and the faraway look in her eye as she spoke about Palobar, but his head was wrapped up in the devil's details of a thousand well laid plans.

"It's kind of funny. So much of the last four years of my life have revolved around him, but he never really registered."

"How so?" she asked, curious about his reaction.

"I didn't really think much of him when we met. I didn't put much stock in his chances of success when we funded him and bankrolled his little war. By the time I signed his death warrant, I could barely remember what he looked like."

Her heart rate spiked and she fought back tears welling up in the corner of her eyes. Her blood boiled like cold water hitting a hot skillet. For a moment, everything in her head felt broken and amplified. His words bounced off the insides of her skull, ringing in her ears. It wasn't just the words, but how little consideration he gave them. It took every ounce of willpower for her not to show her hand.

"You... signed his death warrant?" she asked.

"More or less," he replied, still flipping through aerial photographs of the area. "The agency wanted to destabilize the region, so they authorized us to pay his security detail a ridiculous sum of money to take him out."

"Destabilize the region... why would they want that?" she asked, still struggling with Abe's nonchalant tone. He spoke about execution with no more care than he would ordering a cup of coffee.

"It's pretty simple," he replied, finally making eye contact with her. He immediately knew something was amiss. "Palobar had made assurances about quantities crossing the border. My bosses wanted to control the flow of traffic. Turns out your old boss had been ignoring those requests. At that point, our only option was to remove Palobar, crater everything, and find someone else who was willing to play ball."

Her insides were still brewing. A cauldron of cinders burning brightly. Just four feet across from her was the man responsible for the death of the person she had idolized. The man whom she had pined for and tethered all her hopes and dreams. And he spoke about it as if it was nothing. Even if she could forgive the act, she could not forgive the disrespect. Magdalena had spent her life obsessing about escape. Now her only thoughts were of murder. Her mind would tell her that she needed Abe to locate the vault which would provide her enough money to live a comfortable life free of the poverty she had become accustomed to. Her heart was telling her something else. That she would avenge her fallen idol, slit his throat, and spit on his cold, lifeless corpse.

The storm continued to rage outside, the perpetual sound of dripping water seeping through warped wood. A flash of lightning cast a shadow from the window frame on the far side of the room. A clearly drawn head, torso, and arms.

Instinctively, Magdalena looked for cover, sheltering herself behind Abe. His training was far more ingrained. In one fluid motion, Abe was able to unholster his gun, turn off the safety, and aim at a potential target. By the time the bright flash of light had subsided, whatever had been there was gone.

"Stay here," said Abe, moving towards the window.

Through the window he could see very little. The pitch black skies and steady pour made details difficult. He could see the trees lurching back and forth in the wind.

"It's nothing," he said, chalking it up to happenstance.

Carl patrolled the hall and noticed Aren emerging from a room at the far end.

"Everything all right?" asked Carl.

"Yes, yes. Everything's fine," he replied. "It's just that… where's the bathroom in this place?" he asked.

"You're out of luck there. They've all been stripped bare or left in ruin. Cartel guys like to hide stuff in toilets and the hollows of fixtures, so they took a sledgehammer to all of it."

"So where am I supposed to…" said Aren, not wanting to finish the sentence.

"Normally I'd say outside, but in this weather I'd say find an empty room and go to town."

Aren's lips pursed and his eyes squinted. That was not the answer he was hoping for.

"Though I'd recommend finding a room away from where we're holed up. You know, to avoid any… inconvenient odors."

Aren slowly made his way through the house, tiptoeing across every creaky floorboard. He targeted a room at the far corner of the house for both privacy and consideration. At one point this had been the master bath. The fine porcelain had been reduced to rubble. The room had a depression in the middle where a bath had once rested but was now nothing more than a hole with exposed pipe fittings.

At this moment, Aren may have been willing to part with his share of the take for a functioning toilet. This hole would have to do.

He dropped his pants, squatted down, and closed his eyes in an effort to relax himself and expedite the process. The sound of the wind pushing through a nearby window frame was distracting him, forcing him to cup his hands over his ears. All the effort to shut down his senses prevented him from noticing an intruder crawling up into the house. Through his muted ears, Aren heard a noise. He refused to open his eyes immediately, instead slowly lifting his lids until he could make out the barest of details. Someone was perched in the window frame staring down at him.

With no real survival instinct, Aren froze. This was becoming more difficult as his legs began to tire and wobble. Eventually he would have to move. Though he wouldn't move his head, he slowly moved his eyes left until he could make out more detail of the intruder. His silhouette was thick, and his eyes pitch black. In the pauses between gusts of wind he could hear heavy breathing. Aren followed the sounds of breathing to its mouth. There he could see the teeth. No, not teeth. Fangs.

Another bright flash of lightning filled the room. Aren then realized the intruder was something other than human. The clap of thunder that followed snapped Aren from his paralysis as he bolted for the door. He ran down the hall as fast as he could, his pants still balled up around his ankles. His panicked cries were loud enough to be heard throughout the house.

"Who's that?" barked Abe, emerging from his

room.

"Aren," replied Carl, running towards the sound of his screams.

Aren ran fast enough and with enough momentum to bowl over Carl as he came around the corner.

"It's behind me!" he yelled frantically. "I think it's behind me."

"What's behind you?" asked Abe, moving Aren out of the way and scanning the hallway.

"Something came in through the window," he said, trying to catch his breath. "Black… with teeth…"

The words made little sense and Aren was so gripped with fear that he could only muster to repeat them.

"Black… teeth."

Then it appeared at the far end of the hall, walking through the door as if it owned the place, eying the intruders and defiantly walking towards them.

"Can I get a light down there?" asked Abe.

Carlos obliged by lighting a halogen flashlight affixed to his assault rifle. The bright light filled the chamber. On the other side was a chimpanzee. Like the other animals they had encountered, something was off. Its eyes were blood-red, and his body was draped in gray skin where thick black hair had once been. The strong beam was blinding. Most animals would have fled. Not this one. He merely lowered his head and growled, showing off the fangs that had turned Aren into a frightened puddle.

"It's just a monkey," said Carl, chambering a bullet into his pistol. "And not even a cute one. You want me to kill it?"

"No," said Magdalena. "Why would you want to

hurt an innocent creature? "

"He doesn't look all that innocent," replied Carl.

It's not a monkey, it's an ape, " said Nil.

As the ape looked up, they could see a dried red smear across its scowling face.

"Is that blood?"

Without trepidation, it fearlessly took a few steps forward.

"What's it doing?" asked Carl, amused by the fearless ape.

"I think it's trying to let us know we're the houseguests in this scenario," said Nil.

"If he wants a pissing contest, I got plenty," replied Carl, wrapping his finger around the trigger.

It continued to pace back and forth. A line had been drawn. The beast would not be intimidated by these tourists.

"I don't know about anyone else, but I'd sleep a lot better knowing that thing wasn't walking around the house waiting to kill me in my sleep," said Nil, pulling out his revolver.

"Enough," said Abe, ending the discussion, pulling out a signal flare from his satchel and lighting it.

The orange flame surged forth as Abe moved towards the ape. Its stoic silence was abandoned as it shrieked and slammed its fists into the ground.

"Get out while I'm giving you the chance," yelled Abe, waving the flare back and forth.

The ape slowly backed away from the light and into the darkness. With one wave of the torch it was there, and the next it was gone, receding into the shadows. Like all good soldiers, Abe was not content with the baboon simply being out of sight.

He followed it into the bathroom, looking out the open window. In the distance he could make out the faintest detail of the animal navigating the branches of the nearby trees, making its way away from the house. Abe thought back to the field reports that had listed the property as abandoned. Perhaps those assessments had been premature.

CHAPTER TWELVE

Sergio Lourdes was the kind of crass opportunist who thrived in the filthy shadows of the civilized world. He had made himself indispensable to a number of international criminal enterprises by delivering whatever was needed by anyone willing to cut him a check. There was never a judgement or any inference of difficulty. Sergio delivered whatever was asked of him without question. To date, no situation had been presented that was beyond his means. Whether that be the procurement of illegal goods and services, discreet movement across international borders or securing leverage over public officials. His penchant for being able to obtain anything had garnered him the nickname 'The Concierge'.

Raul Paolobar had been a client for many years. A perpetual blank check whose requests quickly moved everyone else to the back burner. While the money was always a motivating factor, it was the peculiarity of Palobar's requests that intrigued the Concierge. While many of his clients requested guns, drugs or labor, there were precious few who asked for fully functional submarines and industrial tunneling machinery. Palobar's requests often presented a challenge that eluded the Concierge in the vast majority of his dealings.

His eyes lit up like a child when he received a call to help assemble a functioning zoo in the heart of the

South American jungle. This was the kind of eccentric job filled with so many delicious layers. The concept of assembling a private zoo from scratch was the kind of cognitive challenge he craved.

The physical structures were purchased and smuggled into the country from a shuttered zoo and accompanying water park from the former Soviet Union. The recent collapse of the superpower had become an international flea market where anything and everything could be acquired. Unfortunately, most of the animals had already been sold off to other zoological enterprises from around the world. Filling the cages would be significantly easier than acquiring them.

There were a number of resources readily available in his backyard. Bird and monkey poachers were already a known commodity throughout South America. He was able to purchase a variety of larger African animals from poachers. Lions. Tigers. Even a handful of hippopotami. Japanese dolphin hunters were willing to part with a number of their prey for a hefty price. A few advantageous American businessmen were willing to 'misplace' a number of infant sharks to give the aquarium some teeth.

The only item that eluded him were the big apes. Many gorillas had become endangered in recent years, the populations protected not only by Governments but by environmental groups making their acquisition difficult, even by the Concierge’s standards. He finally made some headway after reaching out to a number of hunters in Central Africa. One of them claimed to have a 'freak ape' that had been plaguing villages for years. A stray that made potential buyers nervous due to its unruly nature. Even the pharmaceutical companies who contracted his services looking for animals for laboratory testing were uninterested due to its grotesque appearance. A combination of alopecia and scar tissue made him an unsettling proposition.

The Concierge exhausted every other available resource. But Palobar was on a specific timeline, moving heaven and earth to ensure his daughter's wish would come true. Had there been more time, a better option could have been found. However, the Concierge's most valued client was on a crucial timeline and the thought of disappointing him was something he refused to consider.

CHAPTER THIRTEEN

The group was assembled and ready to inspect the grounds by first light. There was an energy, an eagerness that motivated every one of them.

"Here're the rules," said Abe, sliding his sunglasses on. "We stay together. No one ventures off, no one splits from the group. Do we understand?"

"We will take scheduled breaks," he continued, walking down the line inspecting them one by one. "In the efforts of saving time, we break every two hours. You piss in pairs."

"Why?" asked Magdalena, somewhat uncomfortable with the concept.

"Because there are still a number of intangibles and I don't want anyone isolated. Isolation makes it easy for whatever is out there to pick us off."

"What is out there?" asked Aren, somewhat nervously. "What are you worried about?"

"I'm worried about the uncontrollable, Mr. Brecht. If I keep us together, if everyone has a pair of eyes on one another, then I have nothing to worry about. The third rule is, stay hydrated. We located a well, so there's plenty of fresh water. Make sure you're drinking at least sixteen ounces every two hours. Good?"

The group half-heartedly responded, like a group of students on a field trip only partially paying attention to their teacher.

"Carlos and Christian, you're on point. We don't do blind corners, people. When you see Christian and Carlos stop, you stop. We wait for the signal, and we proceed.

"The last rule, and this is the most important," he said, pausing for effect. "We do not panic. If you see something that requires our attention, you do not make it audible. You don't scream or yell. You calmly get the attention of myself, or my associate and we will make sure it is dealt with. The moment you panic is the moment you give up your tactical advantage. We are well prepared, armed to the teeth, and have a working knowledge of the location. If we keep our composure and avoid exposing ourselves, we will accomplish this mission sooner rather than later."

It was the same speech he had given a hundred times before. Abe believed in certain non-negotiables on any mission he undertook. Preparation. Mitigating risk. Formulating well researched back-up plans. Strategy was something he excelled at and took great pride in. Planning for every eventuality wasn't just a skill, it was a passion.

With a tactical plan laid out, the group exited the house and took the lush, overgrown grounds that spiraled from the back of the house all the way to the rocky cliffs that lined the northern Colombian coast. There were hundreds of acres to search. The plant growth made visibility difficult. There were some man-made markers that could be spotted above the tall grass and thin brush. Most notably a stone fence that ran almost the entire length of the property.

"So where do we start?" asked Carl.

"There's a number of buildings in the back of the

property. Stables. A guest house. Servant's quarters. We're looking for something small. A door, a hatch, something that would lead underground. Since it's not in the main house, my money is on it being in one of the other dwellings."

"And what if it isn't?"

"Then we break out the metal detectors and start scanning the property inch by inch."

"Lovely," replied Carl.

The stables were barely standing. Only the framework remained. At one point they had housed some of the best purebred horses on the continent. Like anything of value, they were liquidated with every asset Palobar had ever acquired.

Magdalena was the only one still capable of seeing the luster, looking at everything with a childlike innocence. In her mind, she saw the property in its pristine state. Thoroughbred horses galloped along the wide open expanses and young children fed small ponies carrots. For her, it was still a place of dreams. Delusion was all she had left.

The initial search of the grounds was uneventful. The kind of rank and file military operation that favored a metered pace. This was a process, the kind of search and seizure that Abe and Carl had run their entire career. Systematically move across a grid in an orderly fashion crossing off potential targets before moving on to the next.

After moving through the main residences of the compound, they ventured towards the north side. A large expanse that contained a multi-car garage and racetrack, a shooting range, and a zoo which had housed as many as 40 different species of animals. A single road connected the grounds to the rest of the complex. An overgrown stretch of asphalt that had already cracked and splintered with thick brush growing through.

"Hold," said Carl, surveying the next stretch of land with binoculars. "We've got a gate up ahead."

"Lead in with two. Check left, right. I'll take point," replied Abe, turning off the safety on his rifle.

"It's all so dramatic, isn't it?" said Aren, looking for shade.

"Wouldn't be an army operation without cadence," said Nil, watching them take formation.

There was none in this hilly nothing connecting the two properties. It was little more than tall grass which just off the road had grown to great heights.

They approached the gate single file. Up front, Abe could see the gate had been torn away at the hinges. The rusty hinges still clung to the pieces of stone that had been torn from the wall. Once through the opening, they fanned out into their positions.

"Clear," said Carlos.

"Clear," said Christian.

"Clear," said Abe, finishing the trifecta.

"Well, we're all clear," said Carl, bringing up the rear. "That has to be comforting."

"I thought you were a military man," said Magdalena.

"Don't let the tactical gear fool you," replied Nil. "I'm strictly freelance, and I'm not a big fan of brainwashing or group think."

"How has that worked out for you?" she asked.

He craned his neck and turned to look at her with his one good eye.

"I'm still here, ain't I? The good parts anyway."

"Stay sharp," said Carl, barking over his shoulder

to the talkier members of the party bringing up the rear.

"Clear," said Nil, not even bothering to look over his shoulder.

"What could have done this?" asked Magdalena, looking to the broken gate.

"Maybe an animal. Maybe the ravages of time."

"It's only been a couple of years," she replied.

"Are you familiar with Charlie Chaplin?" Nil asked, lighting a cigarillo. "You know, the silent movie star?"

"I've heard of him," she replied.

"So the guy becomes a big deal in Hollywood, and he decides to build himself a mansion. But he decides to go cheap. Doesn't want to pay a lot of money for it, so he brings carpenters from the movie studio to help build his house. The guys who build the sets and the fake locations."

He paused to exhale a huge cloud of smoke.

"Instead of skilled labor, the guy brings in people who only know how to build fake shit. So what do you think happens?" he asked.

"I don't know."

"Seriously?" he replied. "I thought I telegraphed that pretty clearly. The whole place falls apart. The ceiling starts to crumble. The floors start to sink. The whole place was a disaster waiting to happen. They called it the breakaway mansion."

"What does that have to do with anything?" asked Carl.

Nil kneeled down next to the section of broken wall, picking up a piece of mortar. As he rubbed it between his fingers it crumbled into dust.

"I got a feeling our old friend Palobar was

contracting to the lowest bidder."

"Still, it would have taken something pretty big to take it down."

"What happened to the animals after the place was abandoned?"

"Nothing," replied Abe.

"They just left them here?" asked Aren. "That's horrible."

"If I remember correctly, the remote location made it difficult to find a motivated buyer," said Carl. "That's the story I heard anyway."

"So whatever they couldn't sell they just left here to rot?" said Nil. "That's what happens when the capitalists win."

"You'd prefer the alternative?" asked Carl.

"I'd prefer nothing. Anarchy. Reduce it all to a zero sum and let everything sort itself out."

"Says the man who has nothing." said Abe.

"By choice, you bourgeois pig," replied Nil. "I'm a self-made minimalist."

"Then why are you even here?" asked Carl.

"Because I wanted the chance to piss on Palobar's grave. I wanted to see everything he built in shambles, reduced to nothing."

The ground trembled ever so slightly, freezing everyone in place.

"What the hell was that?" asked Carl.

"Tectonic shift?" asked Abe.

They continued, one after the other, each of them becoming greater in intensity.

"Incoming," yelled Nil.

"Incoming what?" replied Carl.

"And from where?" screamed Abe, trying to be heard over the thunderous claps.

The terrain made it impossible to spot, not until it was upon them. It emerged from the tall grass, a giant gray mass surging forward, its frothing, gaping maw exposing enormous yellow fangs. Most threats were met with reaction. These men had seen battle and were trained to react to any number of scenarios. This was not one of them. This was a crazed wild animal charging right at them. Panic set in and the group began to scatter, moving in any direction that took them out of the path of destruction.

Christian was the slowest to react, choosing defense over retreat. He began to unload his shotgun, but the blunt blasts had surprisingly little impact on the raging beast. The six straight shots had taken chunks out of its hide, but had not even slowed it down. For one brief instant, Christian glimpsed the massive creature that rippled as it raced ahead. The lower teeth punctured his abdomen, tearing through flesh, muscle, and bone as if it were nothing. The jaws clamped down, crushing his ribs. All the breath left him. By the time it had exited, he was gone.

"Christian!" screamed Carlos, watching the whole gruesome event unfold.

The beast stopped, spitting out the mangled carcass of Christian to the ground before turning back around, preparing for another volley. For the first time, they could see its bloodshot, beady eyes.

"It's a fucking hippopotamus," said Carl, somewhat shocked by the revelation. "A hippo just killed Christian."

"Thanks for the color commentary," said Nil, dusting himself off and arming up. "How about we put a little intention behind it and kill the hippo that just killed Christian."

Carlos had already entertained this notion, fighting back the anger welling up within him, salient enough to taste and smell. He unloaded the entire magazine of his assault rifle. Thirty-six bullets pierced its hide, but it barely registered. The angry hippo shook its head back and forth as it recoiled.

"Carlos, get out of the way!" yelled Nil trying to line up a shot.

His bloodlust had shut down his senses. This hippo was going to die by his hand. The small space between the chamber emptying and his reload reflex kicking in was enough for the hippo to charge forward. Carlos would not change course, firing at will into an animal who seemed to either lack or have passed its threshold for enduring punishment.

"How's your curveball?" said Abe, tossing a grenade to Carl.

"There's two on, bottom of the ninth…" he replied, pulling the pin and winding up like a big league closer.

Carl had been living this fantasy since he was eight years old where he pictured himself playing for the New York Mets with Gary Carter on the other side of the plate. Over the years he had developed a fairly accurate aim. With Carlos impeding his line of sight, the only option he had was to go up and over.

"I'm gonna have to go with a sinker on this one, " he said before tossing the explosive.

It was a perfect throw soaring above Carlos who screamed while firing his assault rifle, so gripped by his rage that he didn't even notice the grenade ricochet off the roof of the hippo's mouth and down into its throat. The subsequent blast emerged from its esophagus like a cannon, the shockwave slamming into Carlos with the impact of a mortar. Like a closed fist holding a firecracker, the rest of the blast had nowhere to escape, tearing through the hippo's midsection, splitting it in half and spraying a combination of blood and bile into the air which rained down onto a half-conscious Carlos.

"Come on!" said Carl, jumping into the air celebrating his strikeout. "Right across the plate."

"Not the time, Carl," said Abe, staring at the speared remains of Christian's lifeless body.

"As far as ways to go, that was unique," added Nil.

"Not helping," replied Abe. "Why don't you go help Carlos."

Carlos was beyond traditional help. He wiped the detritus from his face and pulled himself to his feet, walking through the remains of the scattered entrails of the hippopotamus. When he stumbled upon the mutilated head he fell to his knees and stared deeply into its hollowed out eye sockets. With no other readily available target for his anger, he clenched his hands into fists and began to strike the severed hippo head repeatedly. Mashing his fists into the pulpy remains of his fallen foe. A futile act perpetrated by a man who only understood violence.

"We better get a lid on this quick," said Carl. "Keep moving before this gets messier."

"No," replied Abe. "We do this right."

Abe and Carl dug the hole while Magdalena offered comfort. Carlos knelt before his brother's lifeless body wrapped in some old burlap found near the barns. He clenched his fists and eyes offering up the Lord's Prayer over and over again, only pausing to take a swig of liquor from his flask and wash down the handful of prescription pills that were keeping him from shattering. They would lay his corpse in a shallow grave near the broken gate. Carlos took his blood-soaked hand and scrawled a single word on the stone wall.

"Sin sentido," said Carlos, still trying to clean away the remains from his face.

"There's a building up ahead," said Carl to Abe. "Maybe we should stop, let everybody catch their breath."

The zoo was laid out like any other with a main building that served as a hub for the facility. Ticket booths, an ice cream parlor, and even a gift shop. To the naked eye it was no different than the welcome center of any mid-sized theme park.

"What is this?" said Nil, feeling slightly out of place.

"When you said 'a zoo', I was thinking like a petting zoo," added Carl. "You know, some goats and maybe an orangutan."

A large sign hung over the main entrance. The paint had been stripped away and some of the letters had started to detach from their moorings.

"Alomenia?" said Aren. "Who is Alomenia?"

Magdalena looked at the sign and smiled.

"She was his daughter."

CHAPTER FOURTEEN

Raul Palobar loved his children. They were his simplest pleasure. He had grown up with nothing, practically orphaned at an early age with no ties to his family. As he rose to power and prominence, he made sure his family benefited. His money existed to provide them with the kind of childhood he had never known. They were educated by the finest tutors, taken on frequent trips to all corners of the globe, and given lavish gifts with great frequency.

Palobar loved all his children. He respected the men his sons had become. They were strong and fearless. His oldest, Juan, studied in his father's footsteps to one day take over the family business. Antonio, his second son, lacked the hard discipline that his business required. He never had the stomach to deal with the raw brutality of his father's chosen field, and so he turned his attention to the poor and would devote his life to the Lord and his suffering servants. Every dime his father bestowed upon him would be used to build churches and feed the hungry. Even though his father wanted a different life for Antonio, he valued his choices. The fact that his son helped feed and clothe the poorest barrios where he had grown up brought him a sense of accomplishment. Though he loved his two sons, it was his daughter Alomenia that was the light of Fernando Palobar's life. She would smile the moment he entered the room. Her laughter filled him with a warmth he had not known since his earliest days. Alomenia was everything to Palobar. She was his world.

When she became ill, he brought in the finest doctors and specialists from around the world. Their treatments could not cure her. Then he turned to experimental medicines and the healing arts of Eastern culture. They were equally ineffective. He would have leveraged his entire fortune to save her. The billions at his disposal were meaningless if his children had to suffer. After the terminal prognosis had been made, when he realized there was nothing more he could do for her body, he turned to her spirit.

Alomenia had always loved animals. No matter what city they travelled to, the zoo was where she wanted to go first and the moment she left, she asked her mother and father when they could go back. When Alomenia could no longer go to the animals, Palobar arranged an alternative. This zoo was his living tribute to his beautiful daughter who had enriched every day of his life. It would be just like the zoos in the cities she had visited down to the last detail. Filled with every animal she had ever wanted, built brick for brick to recreate the experience.

When it was first completed, he would walk with her down the cobblestone walkways for hours, watching her face light up at the sight of these treasures he had imported solely for her enjoyment. As she grew weaker, he would wheel her to her favorite destinations, still able to catch glimpses of her fleeting happiness. Towards the end when it became difficult, he would have the handlers bring some of the animals to her room. She loved them all, but her favorite was a hairless chimpanzee that she had nicknamed Ceno, for the frown he always seemed to wear.

Those closest to Palboar said that Alomenia was his tether to this world. That the little good in him was buried along with his beautiful daughter. There were no more ties, no more emotional investment, and no reason to live under the guise that he was a good man. The hole left by Alomenia was replaced with an insatiable greed and lust. He would bury himself in his business and soon became addicted to the product he peddled. His descent into avarice, the disintegration of restraint, the dark descent that would lead to his inevitable demise was all a product of his loss. In his final years, he barely visited his palatial estate, the dream home he had built, which had become little more than a sobering reminder of her absence: a monument to his suffering.

CHAPTER FIFTEEN

Forward momentum. It's the most important component of any plan. Abe and Carl made sure to keep everyone in formation and venturing forth. Christian's death was a random act of absurdity that had already drastically changed the dynamic. Carlos and Christian were intentionally brought on board because of their lack of emotional investment. Nil, Magdalena, and Aren all had connections to Palobar. Their judgement could not be counted on. Now that his brother was dead, Carlos had become another potential liability. This thought troubled Abe, who had accounted for just about every potential variable. Murderous zoo animals had not been something he considered.

"That smell..." said Aren, pinching his nose with two fingers. "Can't he walk behind us?"

"Suck it up," replied Nil. "The man's got a job to do. Let him do it."

Carlos still held the point. The dried blood and entrails had stained him red, leaving behind a pungent odor for those around him.

"There's some structures about a kilometer ahead," said Carl. "Stay alert, and be ready for anything."

With their focus on what lay ahead, there was little attention paid to what was behind them, slowly amassing in the skies above. Nil was the first to notice the shadows cast on the surrounding ground. At first only one or two, but rapidly multiplying.

"Hey, boss," said Nil. "You seeing this?"

Abe and Carl both looked back. Nil motioned with his barrel straight up to the sky, pointing out the handful of vultures circling the group.

"Vultures?" said Carl as he held his hand to his head trying to see them through the bright beams of the midday sun.

"Carrion," replied Nil. "I expect they caught a whiff of the mess we made back at the gate, and now they're following our scent."

"I don't think it's anything to worry about," said Abe.

The numbers continued to multiply, each one of them joining in the circular flight pattern overhead. As their ranks grew, so did their audacity, squawking loudly into a piercing chorus. Shedding feathers began to descend from above as they began to fly faster and more frenzied.

"I think we seriously have to reconsider what we do and don't need to worry about," said Carl.

"Up ahead," barked Carlos. "Cages."

An old wooden sign hung from the guard rail outside the habitat, with the word 'Uakari' carved into the surface.

"What's an uakari?" asked Magdalena.

"Monkeys," replied Nil. "Little ones."

There were none in sight. Inside the caged bars were warped wooden play areas for monkeys.

"So where did they go?" asked Carl.

Nil had not taken his eye off the carrion, who had descended to the ground below and marched behind them, cawing like a Greek chorus.

"What do you think they want?" asked Magdalena.

"Lunch," replied Nil

Suddenly, the birds began to scramble. Some took to the skies while others flapped their massive wings.

"Something's got them spooked."

"Maybe they've never seen people before."

"It ain't us that's spooking them."

They had made their way to the top of the uakari habitat without as much as a sound. Ocelots. A pack of at least ten perched and ready to fight. It was only half a second between the time Abe laid eyes on them and the sight of the first one leaping through the air, over the search party and into the sea of carrion at their backs.

The grounded vultures drew the large cats into their circle as others swooped down from above, making quick, calculated strikes. The ocelots snapped with their fierce jaws and tore through feathered frames with razor sharp claws. The others just stood and watched as these two packs of predators tore into one another.

"It's like God damned Wild Kingdom," said Carl.

"None of this makes a lick of sense," said Nil, who lowered his guard long enough to light a cigarette. "Ocelots hunt and kill… carrion picks the corpses clean. This here... this is unnatural."

"Not that I'm questioning your anthropological skills, but why?"

"Because they don't do this…"

"Do what?"

"Two different levels of the food chain… Killing each other over territory. Nature has a balance… an order... This isn't it. "

CHAPTER SIXTEEN

The welcome center showed the same kind of wear that plagued the rest of the property. The tile walls had cracked and crumbled leaving a layer of powdery debris on the floor. The glass poster displays were shattered or smudged with dirt.

"This might be a good place to take a break and take care of business," said Carl, dropping his supplies. "Everybody take a breather."

Aren and Magdalena spotted the restroom signs and headed to their respective facilities. Nil was systemically incapable of lowering his guard but allowed himself the use of his free hand to procure some rations. Carlos still hadn't broken free of the chemically-induced stupor he used to deal with the death of his brother. He stood stoically in the corner with a blank expression, running his finger up and down the trigger of his assault rifle. To Abe, the shelter seemed like a good place to regroup. Somewhere they would be protected from the elements and clear of the escaped animals that seemed to be lurking in every corner. When it was first built, the aviary had housed some of the most exotic birds on the continent. The ones who had survived starvation and neglect after the property had been shuttered managed to escape through a storm damaged roof. The tall spire at the center of the property served as a gathering point for the various animals that remained.

They could hear them as soon as they entered.

Shrieks and howls echoing off the cylindrical shape of the structure. The aviary had been built to resemble an enormous, four story cage. Each level shrank in size, leading to a large series of perches hanging from the ceiling.

Holes in the well-worn roof shone with beams of light casting shadows against the interior walls. They could be seen gathering at the top, leaping from the high perches to the surrounding balcony. But it was the smell that hit them the hardest. The stench of them collected in that poorly ventilated column. Years of filth collected in every corner. It was thick and foul. For the uninitiated, it was powerful, causing the eyes to tear and the throat to seize up. For those familiar with the odor of death, it was merely unpleasant.

"What's our next move?" asked Aren, struggling to catch his breath.

"This is one of the larger structures in the compound. Check every point on the map for tunnels, doorways, or anything that could lead us to the prize," replied Abe, trying to ensure everyone's focus.

Carlos gripped his assault rifle tightly, running his finger along the length of the trigger. He was still running on raw adrenaline and meth amphetamines, distraught over his brother's death and looking for something to kill. There was still a fire burning deep that needed release.

"Abe," said Magdalena, trying to find a volume loud enough to be heard over the sound of the monkeys but low enough to not be noticed by the others.

He followed her eyes over to Carlos. His pupils

were dilated and his pores were dripping sweat like a leaky faucet.

"Carlos," he said. "You all right?"

He nodded in reply, unable to look him in the eyes, caught in the grip of a debilitating anger.

Nil couldn't look anywhere other than up, staring at the monkeys as they gathered, becoming more and more curious about the visitors that had just invaded their home.

"Let's reload, check our ammunition, and hydrate while we have the chance," said Carl.

The group began to go through their paces. All except Nil who continued to look up into the rafters of the aviary. The shrieks and howls quieted, replaced by an unsettling silence.

"Boss," said Nil while quietly placing a fresh clip into his weapon.

"What is it?" replied Abe, removing some clips from his backpack.

"This might not be the best place to stop."

"Why would you say that?"

"Look up."

Abe looked to see several hundred uakari perched on the roof. The other members of the group followed suit, witnessing what seemed like hundreds of them climbing the walls above, enough of them assembling to block the light emanating from outside.

"We need to move," said Nil. "And move slowly."

"What's the problem?" asked Carl. "They're monkeys. What are they gonna do, fling shit at us?"

"This is their home. We just aggressively entered. They're waiting to see what we do next."

"Seriously?" asked Carl. "This shit is starting to get old."

He pulled out his Uzi and held it high into the air.

"It's time to assert a little dominance," he continued. "Hey! Monkeys! We're gonna camp out here for a little bit, are you ok with that?"

The uakari continued their silent stare. These were not the first humans they had encountered, but the circumstances had changed greatly since the last visitors had come to the zoo.

"What are they doing?" asked Aren.

"They're trying to figure out whether we're friend or foe," replied Nil.

"Friend... foe... I'm the one with the machine gun," said Carl before firing a few warning shots into the air.

The uakari began to scatter, leaping from the perches onto the adjacent balconies. Screams and shrieks began to fill the chamber.

"That's right, run. Get the hell out of here," shouted Carl, taking pleasure in the outburst.

The sounds of the gunfire rattled through the chamber, like cannon fire reverberating up the vortex shape of the building.

"See that?" said Carl, holstering his weapon. "Problem solved."

Then, once again, the howls subsided and the silence crept in. There was movement, the beams of light returning as the perches emptied. Shadows of their outlines cast against the walls. The sounds of scratches and scrapes of a thousand appendages moving en masse, and its rumbles were descending, moving closer to the group.

"I'm not loving that sound," said Aren, inching

back towards the door.

"What's wrong?" asked Magdalena as the sounds grew louder.

"He pissed 'em off," replied Nil. "Which means we should be..."

He was interrupted at the sight of them. A dozen uakari were now blocking the door. They were exhibiting high level tactics. While the majority made noise and distracted them, another group quietly moved into place.

"We're not gonna be able to walk out of here, boys," said Abe while slowly removing his gun.

"Stay calm. They're more afraid of us than we are of them."

"Not likely," said Aren, nervously clutching the antique service revolver.

"It's just a pissing contest," said Carl moving towards the door. "It's anthropology 101. Time to be the alpha male."

He unsheathed his machete and held it up over his head. The uakari reared back and squealed but didn't move from their position still obstructing the exit.

"So you don't respect idle threats," he said drawing his gun. "You need to know I'm capable of bodily harm. Fine."

Carl fired a flurry of shots. The uakari scattered but not before a half dozen were mowed down, the gunfire splintering their bodies and spraying the walls with their entrails.

"I told you to move," said Carl, talking as if these wild animals were capable of logic. "This is what happens when you don't listen."

The small fractures in their psyche were beginning to widen with rapid acceleration. Carl's violent outburst helped fuel the others who were already on edge. It was the push that Carlos needed as he opened fire, unloading his clip towards the surge of uakari that had amassed along the first floor balcony. Each shot from his machine gun thundered like a cannon echoing off the acoustically perfect shape of the aviary. The less aggressive members of the group dropped and covered their ears as Carlos wildly fired towards anything that would move, channeling his loss into wild fury.

"Hold your fire," said Abe trying to put a stop to this madness, but he couldn't be heard.

The clip quickly emptied and the final casing hit the floor. Echoes of the final shots ascending up into the ceiling. Now it was their turn. The uakari emerged from their hiding places taking a moment to survey the dead bodies that now littered every corner. Fear quickly turned to anger. They would not flee. This was their home, and they would defend it with their lives.

"What now?" asked Aren.

"Now we run," replied Nil.

The uakari began to leap from the rafters and balconies, a dozen at a time. These animals recognized a certain type of hierarchy and focused first on Carlos who struggled to reload his gun as four, five, then six uakari fell onto him, scratching and clawing. Their small claws tearing into his flesh, biting with their razor-sharp teeth.

"Which way?" screamed Magdalena, looking to the door. The uakari were already there cutting off their exit.

They were employing strategy. Taking out the biggest threat. Making sure escape was not an option. These were the actions of intelligent creatures.

"They want a fight," said Abe, finally realizing there was no cerebral solution to this scenario. "We give them one."

He dropped to one knee, spinning his backpack off his shoulder and grabbing several pieces, quickly assembling a weapon.

"What's the plan, Abe?" asked Carl while rattling off a few shots.

"Unleash hell," responded Abe. With the flick of a button, a small orange flame emerged from the tip of his whip, and then, a fountain of fire emerged.

The flamethrower sent the uakari scattering back into the rafters, their shrieks loud enough to drown out the ensuing gunfire. Carlos, Carl, and Nil fired wildly into the fleeing monkeys as they trampled one another to try and escape the slaughter. The screams produced were the stuff of nightmares, the sight of them burning, the smell of them as they slowly cooked. This would haunt them for as long as they lived whether that be hours, days, or years.

The final flames flickered from the barrel. The orange glow faded. The blistering heat subsided.

"Be the Alpha male, huh?" said Abe mocking Carl. "Assert a little dominance, he says."

"Better than doing nothing," he replied.

"That's debatable," said Nil surveying the damage. "This is wrong."

"You're just figuring that out?"

"These monkeys, they're not normally aggressive."

"I think we've moved beyond normal, Nil."

"Why are they still here?" he asked, shaken by the

strange happenings around them.

"What do you mean?" asked Carlos, wiping the blood away from his wounds. "It's a zoo."

"The cages are broken. Everything is overgrown. They could have cleared out ages ago. And yet, here they are."

"What are you saying?" asked Aren, trying to shake the shiver that was working its way down his spine.

"I'm saying there's something keeping them here. And whatever that is, we should be afraid of it."

They attacked without provocation. No one in the group would consider themselves well schooled in the veterinary arts or had any real experience in zoology. These animals were behaving erratically, exhibiting signs of desperation and paranoia.

"I don't get it," said Carl, surveying the property. "I thought they were supposed to be docile."

"Maybe the isolation got to them?" asked Aren, always looking for a scientific explanation.

"What's keeping them here?" Magdalena asked, looking at a piece of rusted chain wrapped around an open gate.

"The bars?" said Carl sarcastically.

"Some of them, sure," she said, running her fingers along the length of the chain. "What about the monkeys? The ocelots? The peacocks? They could be long gone by now, but they're still here."

It was a good question, one that no one could answer.

"I don't care what's making them act crazy," said Abe, reloading his gun. "I just want to make sure it doesn't get between us and what we're after."

"So what's our next move?"

"We go here," said Abe, pointing to a large silo on the map, then looking up to the structure poking out above the overgrown fauna. "It's the second biggest man-made structure here, after the aviary. There's a high probability our access point is here."

Something stirred behind the wall of flame and smoke. One remaining animal that wouldn't be scared away, not even by the threat of imminent death. Abe could only make out the barest of features, all of them familiar. The amber eyes, the pointed teeth, the grotesque sight of its hairless skin. The confrontational ape they had seen at the residence. It was in the aviary watching this horrific scene unfold, letting out a shriek that alerted everyone to its presence there.

"What the hell is happening here?" asked Carl.

"I don't know," replied Abe. "But I think maybe we need to expedite our timeline."

CHAPTER SEVENTEEN

The silo, like much of the compound, had been intended to require sporadic interaction from the outside world. The facilities required to house such a large stash of supplies and food stores didn't exist. No conventional method existed, leaving the architects to develop creative solutions for these problems. The need was clear: create a large storage depository economical in shape and size. A silo seemed like a logical choice. A large building that could facilitate feedings at 360 degrees and be filled with months of feed that would accommodate a number of different species.

The large cinder block silo had been built from the blueprints of a cattle company, the kind used in conventional farming. This region had become a magnet for cattle farming with thousands of acres of rainforest razed to help produce low cost beef. It was the closest equivalent they could find. After being deemed too small, the proportions were exaggerated to hold the necessary supplies.

Eight stories tall with doors on every side lined with troughs. A lever system used to release the food. Each side stocked with a different type of feed. In the absence of caretakers, the animals had been forced to fend for themselves. Most of the mechanisms had been damaged. Food trickled out from broken chutes to the ground, gobbled up by a handful of wild dogs pushing back and forth to get to the low grade meal. The craftier and more agile animals were able to navigate into ventilation ducts that ran up the length of the building. As they approached, Carl could see a number of uakaris making their way in and out of an air vent. This was the feeding station for the entire zoo. Whatever food remained was here, making it a draw for many of the animals.

The dogs started to become agitated. They were thin and emaciated, and like every other animal they had encountered, extremely prone to violent outbursts. Two of the larger dogs began to growl and snap, circling one another as conflict loomed. Just before they could engage, whisper quiet shots struck the ground in front of them sending the entire pack scurrying into the brush.

"Glad I brought the silencer," said Carl, finally displaying some forethought.

"What are we looking for?" asked Magdalena.

"The access point would be big. At least two meters wide," said Aren, applying sunscreen to the back of his neck. "There's usually a wheel or lever based locking system."

"So we're looking for a two-meter wide needle in a 1500 acre haystack," quipped Nil as he headed through the compound.

The interior of the silo was marred by harsh conditions and weathered from neglect. The rails to control the influx of animals were rusted and warped. The troughs crushed into the ground. Carl pushed the buttons on the release mechanism. Only a smattering of food pellets fell from the opening above, scattering to the ground.

The water well at the center of the silo was still

full. Several small birds were taking sips. Drops of water leaked through the porous holes in the sheet metal roof dripping into the center.

"Maybe at the bottom of the well?" asked Carl.

"I don't see any form of a drainage system," replied Abe.

"Maybe scuba gear?"

"Unlikely," said Nil, kneeling down and tasting the water. "This is fresh water. I doubt you're going to find anything on the other side of this except limestone."

"How fresh is the water?" asked Aren, pulling out his water bottle.

"Fresh enough for them," replied Nil, motioning to the animals.

Aren started to fill his bottle, taking a quick sip as soon as enough had collected. His face went sour.

"Something's not right," he said, spitting the water onto the ground and wiping his mouth.

"It's fine," replied Nil, grabbing a steel ladle clipped to his belt and collecting a sip. "Wait, that's not quite right."

"I told you," said Aren using a kerchief to wipe his tongue and the inside of his mouth.

"What is that?" Nil asked himself, letting another few droplets collect in the ladle.

"Large structure.... lots of storage," said Carl to Abe. "Might be a perfect hiding place."

The only way to the top was a narrow metal ladder that rattled with every step. Carlos advanced slowly, a mag light clenched between his teeth. The shaky beam cut was barely powerful enough to cut through the darkness. The constant dripping sound echoed through the steel cylinder.

"Slow and steady," yelled Carl.

At the top of the silo was a steel door with a rusted padlock holding it shut.

"It's locked," yelled Carlos, barely intelligible with the flashlight in his mouth.

"I'm not sure if this ladder is OSHA compliant," said Carl, ascending the ladder with a pair of bolt cutters in hand.

"I'll file a motion with the union," Abe replied.

The old rusted bolt required precious little pressure to cut. The door provided more of a challenge. The weathered hinge barely buckled. Carlos wrapped his arms around the bars of the ladder to hold himself in place, using the leverage to invert himself and kick at the door. The loud clangs rattled the metal siding, making the whole structure shake.

"That's what I love about the CIA," said Nil, having to yell to be heard over the thunderous noise. "You guys understand the importance of stealth."

After a dozen kicks, the door finally gave way. Carlos' boot had split the rusted hinge. The door swung open and the contents of the silo began to descend to the ground below: a cascade of paper raining down to the bottom of the silo, each piece a different shape and size, catching the air and descending like snowflakes.

"What is it?" yelled Abe.

"God only knows," yelled Carl, shielding his face with his hand. "But whatever it is, it smells terrible."

The first pieces began to land. Some of them collected in Magdalena's hair. It was a familiar shade of green. Abe reached out his hand as pieces began to accumulate. They were no larger than a stamp. He sifted through them, his eyes locking onto a familiar sight: the crest of the Federal Reserve.

"It's money!" shouted Abe.

Carl still clenched one hand over his nose and mouth trying to block the stench emanating from the open silo door. He grabbed a larger piece near the opening. It was torn and frayed, but unmistakable: Benjamin Franklin's face staring back.

"Shredded money?" asked Carl. "Who would shred money?"

Carlos shined the flashlight into the opening. Something caught the light and flickered in the deep background. Then another, and another, multiplying like stars populating a dusky night sky.

"Hay algo allá arriba," said Carlos.

"Did you catch that?" asked Carl.

"He said there's something up there," said Magdalena.

"Can you be more specific?" asked Abe.

"Que Ves?" shouted Magdalena.

Carlos clutched the flashlight in one hand, reaching into the door with the other, pulling his head into the exposed opening. Now inside the dark opening, he immediately saw the perpetrators. Plural. Bats. Rows of nocturnal predators cascading up and into the darkness. Each of their eyes opened and their wings began to open. Their slumber quickly turned to thoughts of survival as they let go of their perched positions and flooded the opening en masse.

They swarmed Carlos, their small frames hitting him with enough force to push him back. As the numbers of fleeing bats grew, his grip lessened. Eventually they overwhelmed Carlos, knocking him from the ladder. The crowd below scattered as the nocturnal predators looked for an exit and Carlos descended some thirty feet to the ground, the sound of his snapping spine masked by the screeching of the bats.

Carl approached Carlos who winced in pain while Abe focused on the ladder, climbing up to where Carlos had been to get an unobstructed view of the interior of the water supply tower.

"No puedo sentir mis piernas," whispered Carlos through clenched teeth.

"He says he can't feel his legs," Magdalena replied.

Abe shined his light up into the tower, the light reflecting from items wrapped in weathered plastic sheeting riddled in holes and tears. The old metal framework of the water tower leaked water into and through these stored items. He ascended higher into the interior of the tower onto a shoddily made platform where he could stand. Using his knife, he poked a hole deeper into one of the plastic-wrapped packages. Inside was a wet white substance that he immediately recognized.

"Jesus…" said Abe to himself before raising his voice to be heard by everyone below. "It's cocaine."

"Not all that surprising given where we are," said Nil, always looking to be the voice of reason.

"It looks like the water has been pouring through it like a god-damned coffee filter."

"So the drinking water is spiked with cocaine?" said Aren, connecting the dots.

"Coked up zoo animals," said Nil with a sarcastic smile on his face. "Well that's a new one."

"It explains their behavior," said Magdalena,

looking for any semblance of reason in this rapidly devolving nightmare scenario.

"We've got other problems," shouted Carl, still trying to work out a plan of action.

Abe emerged from the opening and descended the ladder. He stared at Carlos for a moment.

"Can he move?"

"He says he can't feel his legs and based on his shortness of breath, he might have punctured a lung," replied Carl.

"That's unfortunate. But you know what needs to be done."

Carl looked up to Abe, still struggling to contain the raw emotion these encounters had unearthed.

"Seriously?" said Carl.

"He's literally dead weight."

"You'd just let him die?" asked Magdalena, struggling to hide her contempt.

"I'm not a monster," said Abe, reaching down and pulling out his revolver. "No point in letting him suffer."

"That's all he is to you," said Magdalena, tears welling up in the corner of her eyes. "A dog that needs to be put down."

"Jesus Christ, people. Do you remember what were here to do? What do you propose? That we carry his broken body with us and further slow down this operation? Do you want to carry him?"

He looked each one of them in the eye as he disarmed their emotional argument.

"How about you, Nil? Or you, Aren? You up for hauling this guy across the compound and back through the jungle?"

None of them had an answer or wanted the

responsibility.

"That's what I thought. Everyone's a saint until you ask them to carry the cross."

Abe kneeled down next to Carlos and held up his gun.

"You want to do it or do you want me to do it?"

Carlos looked at the gun and then back to Abe. Carlos took the gun and nodded his head, aware of how dire the circumstances were.

"Good man," Abe said, giving him a reassuring pat on the shoulder. "Time to go."

Abe walked away from Carlos, taking a moment to pull out a kerchief and wipe the second hand sweat and blood from his hands. The others relented, but only for a moment. Nil was familiar with leaving dead weight behind. Aren had no stomach for the brutality on display. Carl and Magdalena looked at one another, both less happy about leaving behind someone they considered 'one of their own'. Carl was never comfortable losing men under his command while Magdalena struggled with watching another of her countrymen brutalized and left behind in this never ending conflict.

Abe turned his back on Carlos and walked a few steps away to give the man some privacy as he took his own life. A single gunshot rang throughout the zoo. The sound bounced off the silo walls like a laughing cacophony, mocking the team for yet another failure. Abe silently cursed himself for his carelessness. Had they been a little more careful, the brothers' uncanny survival record might've gone unbroken. Instead, their years-long lucky streak came to an unceremonious end as the first casualties on what was supposed to be an easy mission.

He didn't get much time to contemplate his mistake, though.

The ground itself began to tremble with a terrible noise the moment that the deafening gunshot broke the years-long silence of the defunct zoo. In his moment of spiteful contemplation, Abe realized a second too late that the noise accompanying the trembling earth wasn't the sound of an earthquake, but the sound of countless galloping hooves crashing against the ground, heading towards them.

Abe dived for Carlos' corpse, intent on getting his gun back and yelled out a warning for the others. "Stampede!"

The silo doors burst open. Over a dozen horses, non-purebred mutts that weren't worth the trouble of acquiring when their owner bit the bullet and left to die in the zoo, stormed into the silo in a coked-up frenzy. Standing on two hands-like feet atop the horse leading the stampede was the hairless ape that was once named Ceno. The insane primate brandished a long white blade that was fashioned out of some poor creature's bone wildly in the air like a cavalryman charging down a hill to route their enemy.

Abe barely managed to touch the handle of his gun with his fingertips before it was kicked away by one of the stampeding horses that proceeded to push him onto his back with a neighing headbutt and run over him, followed by the rest of its friends. Hard, compact hooves slammed into his legs and torso over and over again for what felt like an eternity. Abe was no doctor, but he'd been injured enough times throughout his career to know a cracked rib or three when he felt it. His insides felt like they'd been pounded into mush, and he tried his best to cover his unprotected belly with his arms. Broken bones he could handle, but a ruptured organ would be a death sentence in a place like this.

A glimmer of hope came when Abe noticed one of the horses that still had the remnants of a leather saddle wrapped around the center of its body. It must've been wearing it when the zoo was abandoned and no one bothered to take it off before leaving it to die here. With what little remained of his strength, Abe reached out and grabbed the leather strap of the saddle. He held onto the leather in a vice grip as he was dragged away from his group by the horse, tired and bruised but no longer getting trampled.

Meanwhile, Carl, Nil, Aren, and Magdalena ran for their lives out of the silo. They couldn't match the speed and power of the stampeding horses, but being smaller and nimbler had its advantages in this case. While the horses crashed into and tripped over discarded debris or stumbled about for a way around them, the four humans were able to vault over anything in their path with relative ease.

They barreled through the silo door and into the open zoo. Carl lagged behind the rest of the group on purpose. There were probably better ways to stop a stampede, but none of them were as satisfying as what he was about to do to these damn horses. He took a split second to chuck a grenade into the silo filled with rampaging horses before closing the door shut. A smile crept onto his face when he heard it explode, accompanied by a hundred horses whinnying in pain.

He left the silo behind and caught up with the rest of the group. What had once been an education center was now their temporary shelter from the madness outside. Billboards depicting the zoo animals outside during happier times hung slanted on various walls while educational plaques containing fun, but useless animal facts lay in shattered pieces on the filthy floor.

There was nothing of worth to the animals here and the wide open space within it assured them that there was nothing hiding in ambush for them here save for the odd insect here and there.

The four of them stood hunched over with their hands on their knees, panting heavily from the life or death race they'd run. Carl was the first to catch his breath and pulled out a cigarette to calm himself with. Magdalena was the first one to break the silence.

"Where's Abe?"

Realization dawned on their faces as a quick headcount revealed that they were missing one person who should still be alive, though between the horses and grenade he should be as good as dead by now.

"Well shit," Nil said, pulling out a cigarette of his own.

"So it's just the four of us now?" Aren asked in between rapid breaths, though none of his companions could tell if he was hyperventilating from the stress or just tired from running. "What do we do now?"

Carl's eyes drifted towards a map of the zoo hanging askew on a cracked yellow wall. An idea started forming in his head when he read the trivia plaque beside it.

"Well figure something out…"

CHAPTER EIGHTEEN

His head pounded like a hundred hammers clanging against a church bell. The reverberations blurred his vision and he fought off the disorientation that had gripped him since he became separated from the rest of the group. His skin was torn, the bleeding clotted by the debris packed into his open wounds. This was the moment, the depth of the crevice where one has only two options: crawl out or settle in and die quietly. He had been here before, in this dark place where the tortured souls are forced to surge or succumb. More often, he was the one administering the punishment, delivering others to this wretched place. There were days when he would have been comfortable dying. Miserable days choked with stress where he fantasized about wrapping his lips around the barrel of his service revolver. Days without purpose where he questioned his role in this world and the point of this meaningless existence.

But not today. Today he had purpose. Today he had a reason to fight. There was a channel for his rage. Somewhere to direct his anger. A bloody, bile filled well in which he would dive deep into. As he picked himself up, the veneer was slowly removed. He hunched over, his fists and teeth clenched. Logic and reason were subsiding, replaced by instinct and carnality. Every thought turned to bloody retribution. There was no strategy here. No tactics to employ. No strategy that would save him from this cocaine fueled ape tearing its way through the complex. Being the more evolved combatant would not help him here.

The only solution here was to unleash hell. This was the kind of war Abe had never fought. Two monsters on a field of battle ready to engage in the kind of savagery that forged this world. He pulled his two daggers from their sheathes, using the torn shreds of his shirt to secure them to his hands. This was not a fight he would win with his fists.

Ceno dragged his bone blade along the ground as he slowly lurched towards his prey. His blood-red face stuck out in the dark shadows of the habitat. Its black, bloodshot eyes were sunken deep into their sockets. From this distance, it looked like a scarlet skull fashioned upon its hairless, muscular frame.

Though he doubled it in size, there was a ferocity that made it formidable. Humans were built for endurance and stamina. In a competition of how long the two of them could march at a steady pace, Abe might've won. But when it came to short-term use of explosive strength like a knife fight, an ape whose biology had evolved to hunt and ambush in the hostile jungle had every conceivable advantage.

Even his knives weren't much of an advantage since the ape had somehow managed to get a blade of his own too. It was only bone and would wear down much faster than his own tempered steel knives, but Abe would already be dead by the time it started to crack. However you looked at it, he lacked the barbarity to win this fight.

An old adage rang through Abe's mind. He couldn't remember who said it, if anyone at all, but it seemed to be fitting advice considering the situation.

When outmatched, cheat.

Abe put one foot behind him and pointed his knife at the hairless ape with one extended hand to warn it to keep its distance while he held his other hand close to his chest for defense. The sight of his knife tip kept Ceno at bay for a few moments. It cautiously paced left and right trying to look for an opening, but Abe followed its movements with the tip of his knife to make sure it knew that it would be skewered if it decided to lunge.

He dug the tip of his back foot into the dirt. It felt soggy against his shoe, which probably meant that some cocaine-infused water had managed to seep into it. That could either be really good or really bad for what he had been planning, but he couldn't think of a better solution if he wanted to survive.

Abe suddenly lowered the knife pointed at Ceno, apparently to ready a stab. As expected, the already tense ape lunged at him the moment it saw an opening. Too bad its attention was too fixed on his knife to notice him kick up the dirt with his back foot until it was too late.

The cocaine water-soaked earth splattered against the ape's exposed eyeballs. It howled at the stinging pain in animalistic rage. Abe dived out of the way of its lunge at the last second. Blinded by the dirt, Ceno didn't realize that its prey had already moved out of the way and plunged its bone blade into the wet earth.

Seeing his opportunity, Abe slashed at the back of the ape's ankle. The blade sliced through the skin easily enough but encountered resistance when it hit bone. He didn't think he'd have the time to reposition himself for a stab in the back and went for the heel instead, thinking that cutting the ape's Achilles tendon would either prevent it from pursuing him or perhaps cause enough pain for it to be stunned.

Unfortunately, he didn't know that most great apes didn't even have an Achilles tendon to cut in the first place. Or that it could still move just fine with help from its muscular arms.

Rage outweighed pain in Ceno's primitive brain. It pulled the bone blade out of the earth and swung it blindly at the direction of the strike which had mangled its heel. The blade alignment was off however, and it only managed to cut a few centimeters into Abe's shoulder before the flat of the blade stopped the edge from digging any deeper. Still, the strike carried with it enough force to rival four human men.

Abe felt his shoulder dislocate from the strike. Meanwhile, Ceno had barely more than a scratch on a limb that it didn't need to beat him to death. If Abe wanted to live to see another day, he knew he had to come up with a new plan and fast.

The ape wiped the dirt from its eyes. Its bloodshot eyes were even redder than before and burned with hatred directed at him. Abe needed another distraction, a bit of dirt wouldn't be enough this time around.

With his good hand, he plunged a knife into one of the ape's bloodshot eyes. The knife easily penetrated the ape's squishy eyeball with a sickening squelch and a squirt as the blood pulsating within the eyeball ruptured out of its severed veins. Ceno screeched in pain again, this time much louder than before as one of its most important assets as a predator was rendered useless forever. Abe immediately hopped backwards just in time to narrowly avoid another vengeful strike from the now half-blind ape. The knife, still connected to Abe's wrist by thin cloth, moved with him and yanked itself out of the ape's eye socket.

He crashed into the ground on his broken shoulder as a shower of high-pressure blood soaked his hair and face. The dislocated bones popped back into place from the impact, more or less. It still hurt like hell, but the adrenaline coursing through his veins allowed him to push through it. He looked up and saw the ape barreling towards him.

Thinking fast, he rolled out of the way on the same side as the ape's now useless eye. The ape crashed into a discarded metal cage, blinded both literally and metaphorically by its own anger. Hiding in the ape's blind spot gave him some more room to breathe, if just barely. His mind raced to come up with another strategy as he scrambled away from the hairless demon before him.

His hand brushed against something hot on the ground while his gaze was fixed upon Ceno wiping the blood off from its eyes. Abe was tempted to ignore whatever it was he'd touched, but in his desperation, decided to risk a look anyways.

Lying on the ground inches away from his fingertips with blood still dripping from its barrel was his gun. The same one he'd handed to Carlos to kill himself with and immediately got lost in a stampede led by the half-blind ape trying to kill him. At that moment, another old adage popped into Abe's mind:

The simplest solution is always the best one.

With no hesitation and the same ease of cracking an egg, Abe picked up his gun and pulled the trigger.

CHAPTER NINETEEN

He stumbled from the cages towards a clearing, collapsing onto a soft patch of earth. In his current state he was barely able to move. Even the simple act of breathing felt as if it took great effort. Circumstances had finally afforded him a chance to recover. No doubt there were still potential dangers around him, but he had exhausted every last reserve. He would be easy pickings for any lingering predators, but he was too tired to care. There he lay atop the dirt and grass. His eyes moved in and out of focus, turning every perfectly imaged blade of grass into a greenish brown blur and then back again. If he were to die here, it would at least be a calm and comforting demise. Here, his last moments would not be in the heat of battle but in the solace of a warm ocean breeze weaving its way through the landscape. It was a far more peaceful death than he had ever expected.

In his current state of paralysis, his view was affixed. Something crept into frame that he could not look away from, something that drew every ounce of his focus. On the ground in front of him was a packet of crackers from his rations, no doubt from one of the many tears to his tactical vest. The crumbs began to attract a few ants rapidly advancing towards this new food source introduced into their ecosystem. The portion was scarce. A fraction of a crumb, barely enough for one of them to eat, much less the six circling the prize.

It took but an instant. The moment of realization between each of the ants that only one could walk away with this prize. Then, the frenzy started. The ants attacked one another, tearing one another apart with their mandibles. Within seconds, legs had been ripped away from their torsos rendering a handful of them immobile. They flailed and fidgeted, trying to get back into the fray but were no longer capable. What had been six ants was now down to two. The most ferocious of them in one last rally to see who would walk away with the spoils of war.

In his current state, Abe had no other option than to watch as these seemingly passive insects had devolved into a murderous frenzy. Even on this quiet, peaceful plain there was conflict. Wars being fought on a battlefield no larger than a few blades of grass. No doubt on those ants were bacteria too small to be seen by the human eye consuming one another in an effort to extend their microscopic life span a few more moments.

In this broken moment he had his epiphany. Life is conflict. At every conceivable level there was a battle being waged. The man fighting for his life to win the gilded cup. The ape protecting his found stash of cocaine from intruders. The ants willing to disarm one another for a speck of food. Everything that inhabits this Earth was born into a state of conflict happening all around us. Life and death being waged in the skies above and the waters below.

Abe was not prone to these kinds of lofty philosophical thoughts. He had never sought any connections to the world around him. Most would find this discovery calming or profound. To Abe, it was merely a blunt truth that yielded one important reality: those who don't fight, die. It was the push he needed. His blood pressure rose, he embraced the aching pains that forced his numb limbs to creak and bend. A deep breath gave him fuel, and he found the will to rise to his feet.

He took one last look at the ant who had claimed his prize and marched back to his home. His options seemed obvious: walk away with the prize or wretch on the ground and wait to die.

Abe had won his prize. And that prize was his life, being able to walk away from a situation that few would've survived and most would love to tell over and over again as exaggerated drunken bar stories. He would've liked to win something worth a bit more than his own insignificant life, but he'd take what he could get.

Injured, exhausted, and suffering from an internal existential crisis, Abe trudged through the zoo and pushed himself into the only building with a door still intact. Almost immediately he heard very human-sounding gasps that made him snap his head up. Carl's familiar voice filled the barren building and for once Abe was glad to hear it.

"Jesus Christ, Abe."

Magdalena rushed to his side and not a moment too soon. Abe's knees buckled and gave way the minute she managed to hoist his arm over her shoulder.

"You are one tough bastard, you know that?" Magdalena almost sounded impressed.

"I've survived worse," said Abe, a wisp of a grin on his battered face.

"Good, " Nil said solemnly. "Because I got a feeling we got more 'worse' coming."

CHAPTER TWENTY

The plan had merit. Palobar had tried to create a self-sufficient estate as well as a bunker where he could hold up for months, if not years. This far removed from civilization, the entire complex was run by a series of kerosene generators. A complex network of pipes had been laid underneath the property connecting large reservoirs of fuel.

"I wouldn't call it a finesse move," said Carl, pointing to various locations on the map. "But we could use these fuel reserves to burn a path across the compound, smoke everything out between us and them."

"Let's call this plan B then?" said Abe.

"So we're sticking with Plan A?" asked Nil.

"Yes," replied Abe.

"What's plan A?" asked Aren, nervously lighting a cigarette.

"Continue ahead on foot, deal with these incursions as they come."

"Can we take a vote?" asked Nil.

"No," replied Abe. "This is a work for hire position. If we want your input, we'll ask."

"Well, I'll put it on record anyway. I say we blow the lines and send these coked up monsters back to whatever hell they spawned from."

"Duly noted," said Abe, quickly quelling any signs of dissent.

CHAPTER TWENTY-ONE

Carl ran through the field, barely able to make out any detail. The fire had spread quicker than he anticipated. The bright orange light of the flames was blinding, and he could feel the heat crawling up his back. His grand distraction was more sweeping than he originally conceived. The fuel lines ran further and deeper into the property than he thought. The unused petrol had been lying dormant for years producing flammable vapors that had seeped into the ground. The underground fuel supplies had turned the entire property into a powder keg and Carl had lit the fuse.

Red and yellow flames erupted from every corner of the property, spewing from the ground like a fountain of fire. Every living thing fled the facility. The birds ascended into the heavens through thick black billowing clouds of smoke. The uakari could be heard shrieking and howling in the distance. The ground shook as every hoofed beast galloped to safety.

"You boys can't do anything small, can you?" said Nil, watching the biblical exodus unfold.

Magdalena fought back tears, watching each subsequent explosion reducing this monument to soot and ash. The last piece of Palobar's legacy burned from existence.

"We need to move," said Abe, watching the surreal sight of a hundred different animals scrambling for survival.

One sight in particular drew his attention: a giraffe had become engulfed in fire and kicked like an angry mule. Under normal circumstances these were beautiful, graceful, dignified animals. Now, drenched in napalm, flailing wildly, screaming with a piercing wail rarely heard by human ears, dignity and grace seemed like foreign concepts.

"This must have been what Noah's Ark was like," yelled Nil, barely able to be heard over the commotion.

"Right," replied Aren. "Except Noah was trying to save the animals. Not burn them alive."

"Where we headin' boss?" asked Nil.

"Stick to the plan. Head towards the water."

"There's a lot of real estate between us and the water," replied Nil.

Carl was already a quarter mile ahead, running for his life, dodging fire and animals both large and small. In his blind sprint he had stumbled into a pack of antelope hastily looking for an exit. They were faster, more frightened, and in these numbers were likely to trample him. Unfortunately, in order to survive there was no other direction to move other than forward.

The fiery maelstrom had done the job. Everything with a pulse was now dead, dying, or desperate to escape the inferno. The only compass Carl had to guide him was to run towards anything not engulfed in flames. There was a dark clearing up ahead, the lure of safety calling to him like a Siren's song. As he got closer, he could see the reflections of the flickering fire against its glassy surface. The water was no longer just safe passage, but a necessity: Carl's clothes had caught fire. His skin was beginning to burn. The adrenaline surged as he leapt up onto the guard rail and then dove headfirst into the water. The flames extinguished and his skin began to bubble. Carl was singed but had survived.

Abe and the other members of the search party were able to navigate the area more safely. The escaping animals had cleared a path through much of the debris. The fires still raged, but they were able to make it to the water in half the time. Carl could see their silhouettes backlit by the fire.

"Over here!" he shouted. "Come on!"

Carl fought back the pain. His nerves were raw. The burnt epidermis felt like a thousand nails being hammered into his nervous system. Now, out of harm's way, the adrenaline subsided and the pain increased exponentially. The surface of the water was illuminated with the reflection of dancing flames swirling with the dark black ripples. He attributed the movement in the water to the light show unfolding on its mirrored veneer and the commotion created by his poor man's dog paddle. It became apparent there was something else, something swimming, circling him aggressively, parts of it exposed atop the waking water.

He immediately panicked. It was expected. Anyone who ever spent any time in the water naturally feared the unknown. Instinct and a lifetime of cinema had created a generation immediately fearful of what lurked below the surface. It could have been a shark or a crocodile. Even with the bright glow of the fire, the water was murky and making out any real details was difficult. He tried to calm himself, slowly paddling towards the platform that would lead him to the aquarium.

"It's not a shark," he said to himself between gasps for air, lumbering towards the ladder. "It's probably a dolphin. Some trained dolphin… probably jumps through hoops."

His attempts to calm himself down were futile. The waters continued to quake, the sound of splashing water coming from every side. The dark shadows that circled him seemed to double, then triple. His leisurely breaststroke had reverted to a panicked front crawl as Carl wildly kicked and pulled at the water. He could see the ladder just ahead of him.

Abe, Aren, Nil, and Magdalena arrived at the crest overlooking the man-made lake. From their vantage point, they could see what Carl couldn't: a swarm of dorsal fins moving towards Carl at an aggravated rate.

"Jesus," said Aren, watching the terrible scene about to unfold.

"No...." said Abe, reaching for his gun.

"Don't waste your ammo," said Nil, preparing for the train wreck he would be unable to look away from.

"Carl! Hit the deck!"

Carl knew the code. Something bad was coming, and he was being instructed to get down. That meant he had only one direction to travel: straight down. He took a deep breath preparing to submerge when the first one surfaced. Black eyes, a pointed nose, and row after row of razor-sharp teeth. Down was not just an option but a necessity of survival. He kicked back, pushing off the shark and started to swim straight down. Abe immediately opened fire, spraying bullets into the water. The sharks began to turn sharply and dive.

Even with his eyes open, Carl could see little more than an orange glow above. He could feel the water wake as the sharks swam by and could hear the muffled sound of bullets being fired. His skin burned and the water began to force its way into his lungs. His senses were betraying him one by one. The burns had sent him into a state of shock. The only benefit to his body failing him was the frayed and damaged nerves dulled the pain of the teeth as they sank into his skin.

The slaughter lasted only a few seconds. From the surface, Abe could see the thrashing of their tails as the frenzy ensued.

CHAPTER TWENTY-TWO

The transition from bright sunlight to almost complete darkness was jarring and played tricks on their eyes. There were trails of light and flickering strobes creating a psychedelic stream across their retinas. Cloaked in darkness and with no sense of geography, the senses began to crave stability. Abe tried to find a fixed point to lock onto. The only thing that could be made out in the darkness was a soft blue light in the distance. For a moment he thought it was the byproduct of his vision adjusting to the light.

"Up ahead. The light," said Abe. "Everybody else see that?"

"I see it," said Magdalena, rubbing her eyes.

"Keep moving."

"Because that's been working so well for us so far," said Nil.

"You want to sit in the dark, fine, Nil. I like my odds better if I can see what's going on around me."

Abe ventured forth towards the wall of circulating blue light. As he drew closer and his vision properly adjusted, he could see it for what it was: a massive wall of water held back by glass. The murky water distilled the light from the fire providing a modicum of visibility.

Magdalena stumbled up to the viewing area, locking onto Abe as she tried to find something as a focal point. She saw him staring straight ahead, a blank expression on his face.

"Are you all right?" she asked, making a half-hearted attempt at consolation.

"No," he replied. "I'm a lot of things right now. 'Alright' ain't one of them."

"I'm sorry. I know you two were close."

"Close doesn't begin to cover it."

"He's in a better place now, Abe. He's at peace."

Abe couldn't be bothered to look over, his gaze still straight ahead. There was no reaching him. Not yet. He had suffered an unexpected loss and was fighting back the anger, swallowing the sadness. It was difficult to watch, and so Magdalena turned to the peaceful waters of the aquarium.

"Oh dear God!" she exclaimed, shocked by what they saw on the other side of the glass.

It was Carl, or what remained of him. A cloud of crimson staining the water with pieces of bone and tissue in various states of weightlessness. It was hardly the first horrible thing Abe had witnessed. In his career he had found a workable level of comfort with the disturbing realities of his trade. He had butchered men before. Beaten them, tortured them, cut them into pieces and reduced them into nothingness. Was this his penance? His punishment? An account being settled after years of cruel acts by his hands? The thought had crossed his mind many times in the last few hours. He had committed many sins in his lifetime, but it was all for a cause. This was the closest Abe had ever come to a spiritual encounter. There had never been a pause to review his life or take inventory of his decision making. Up to this point there had never been the need for course correction. Self-reflection was a tool of the weak, a crutch to be coddled by those who lacked the fortitude to handle rough waters.

He could no longer hold back his frustration. Abe was a man who had always believed in the sanctity of planning. He was an agent of order. Unbridled chaos was the one thing capable of working its way underneath his skin. The blood rushed to his head and his fists clenched. His anger needed a target. The dull thud of his closed fists striking the glass bounced off the concrete walls. Each punch split skin and re-opened the abrasions on his hand, leaving a smear across the glass.

"Easy, boss," said Nil, searching for his flashlight. "You gotta pull it together."

The beam of light cut through the darkness, flooding the chamber with detail. Finally, they had a sense of geography.

"What are we looking for?" asked Nil, trying to maintain what little momentum they had.

"The access point would have to be lower than this," said Aren, surveying the room. "Let me see the maps."

Magdalena spread the maps on the ground. Nil provided the light. Aren began to look at the blueprints.

"It wouldn't be anything in plain sight," said Magdalena.

"If we're talking about an escape hatch, how do we even know it was drawn in," said Nil, trying to apply some logic to the conversation. "If the goal was to keep it hidden, there might not be any markers."

"Abe, you still with us?" asked Magdalena.

"Yeah, I'm here," he replied, slowly regaining his composure.

"We don't know what we're looking for."

"Give me a minute."

"I don't know how many minutes we have, Abe," said Nil. "At this point I'm half expecting the doors to burst open and be attacked by a bunch of strung out walruses or some crabs looking for a fix."

"Quiet," said Abe, still staring into the water.

"I thought you company boys didn't go to pieces like this," said Nil, immediately catching his gaffe.

"Bad form," said Aren.

"Stop talking," said Abe, silencing the room.

Once the voices stopped, a lone sound could be heard: a steady drip of water striking the concrete floor.

"I need some light."

Nil turned the hard halogen beam over to Abe's feet. A trickle of water moved just past his boots following the slope of the floor to the center of the room. Abe followed the flow which snaked through the grooves on the floor collecting underneath an information kiosk featuring photos of various sea life.

"Over here," he said, calling the others over.

Three good shoves knocked the sign from its base. Underneath was a large steel grate providing drainage.

"What do they need drainage for in an aquarium?" asked Aren.

"In a regular aquarium, you'd need it for cleaning the floors," said Abe, grabbing the floor plans and looking them over. "You'd need one if this was a real aquarium with crowds and high foot traffic spilling the nine dollar sodas onto the floor. They built this place using the plans from a commercial zoo. Whatever went in there, went in here."

It took three of them to lift it from its resting place. Underneath was further evidence that could only encourage them: a service ladder built into the concrete piping, wide enough to transport someone through. The strong halogen flashlight could barely reach the bottom of the pipe. Though they couldn't perfectly make it out, there seemed to be an old wheel turn hatch on the other side.

"That's gotta be it," said Nil, grasping at the first sign of encouragement.

"Only one way to find out."

The group fanned out, grabbing their supplies, preparing for the deep descent fueled by the smattering of hope this discovery had provided. Magdalena was the first to take to the ladder.

"Take your time. That's one hell of a drop," said Aren, offering her a helping hand.

Their progress was interrupted by a sharp, piercing sound that bounced off the walls.

"What was that?" asked Aren, the only one in the group who understood that silence was golden.

Nil shined the flashlight around the room with one hand, and wrapped his hand around the barrel of his gun with the other. They continued to hear a noise, far lower in volume than the first burst. A scratching, scraping noise that froze them in their tracks. They had little doubt of its origins. Something had followed them in, or was already here. A deranged, feral animal defending its territory. The light moved from corner to corner, their eyes following the apex of the beam, fearing the inevitable predator stalking them.

The sound then began to double and triple, the

scraping sounds elongating.

"There," said Magdalena, pointing towards the glass wall. "I saw something move."

The halogen light shined against the large glass wall exposing a number of cracks weaving across the surface emanating from holes in the glass.

"Looks like... bullet holes..." said Aren, correctly identifying the impact points from Abe's futile attempts to save Carl.

"Move faster," said Abe, the only words he could muster. "Aren, you're next."

Aren moved into the pipe, awkwardly moving down the ladder. All Nil and Abe could do was watch as the glass walls continued to crack and split.

"How long do you think we got?" asked Abe.

"I think that's the kind of question you don't want to know the answer to," replied Nil.

Water began to spew through the open cracks causing a dozen more. The pressure was becoming too much to bear. It was only a matter of seconds before a wall of water came thrashing through the aquarium glass.

"Get the damn thing open."

"I'm trying!" she yelled, trying to turn the hatch wheel. Even in this heightened state she lacked the strength to make it move.

Aren had finally made his way to the bottom to lend a hand.

"It's stuck!" cried Aren, using every ounce of his limited strength.

"Get down there," said Nil to Abe, still monitoring the fissures and cracks that were rapidly multiplying.

Finally, the glass wall gave way with a thunderous clap, flooding the room with water and debris. Abe watched for a moment as the first wave pushed its way across the aquarium floor, followed quickly by the sea life trapped inside. The insidious sharks, still frenzied from the taste of human flesh, flopped into the water which had gone from ankle deep to knee-deep in a matter of seconds. Abe rushed down the ladder trying not to slip. The shape of the room and placement of the drain funneled water into the pipe making the job of navigating the service ladder and opening the hatch that much more difficult.

Nil had witnessed so many unimaginable terrors that the sight of a half dozen half-submerged sharks gnashing their teeth, racing to feast on him hardly seemed novel.

"Get that god-damned thing open!" he screamed, arming up.

In shallow water, unable to submerge most of their mass, the sharks were at a slight disadvantage. The bullets were able to pierce their hide and do substantial damage. This tactical advantage would be short-lived as the water levels continued to rise.

Abe and Aren gripped the wheel, the pouring water making it that much more difficult to open.

"It's not moving!" said Abe, pulling with all the strength he had left.

"Wait," said Aren, shifting his weight and turning the wheel in the other direction.

The wheel turned and the steel bolts receded.

"It's an old German trick... threading the locks in reverse."

"Nil! Get down here!" yelled Abe as Magdalena and Aren made their way inside.

Far easier said than done. The water was pushing him around the room, the dying sharks flailed and snapped, refusing to die quietly. Nil was out of ammunition, relying on his machete to fend off the remaining sharks. He had to carefully time each swing as they emerged from beneath the rising water, swatting them in the nose with the blade. These merciless creatures seemed to feel no pain as the blade cut a bloody swath across the flesh on their face. Nil tried to maintain a sense of geography, stealing quick glances over his shoulder, making sure to not lose sight of the drain.

Aren and Magdalena made their way into the chamber. Abe waited at the door, looking up the pipe for any sign of Nil. The water was getting higher and the chances of anyone else making it were growing infinitely slimmer.

"We need to move," said Aren.

"We give him another minute," replied Abe.

"In another minute the chamber will be flooded, and we won't be able to seal it off," he replied.

Abe had already lost so many on this mission. More than he was comfortable with. He had no problem sending people off to die, but bearing witness to so many dying under his watch had hurt his pride.

"There's nothing you can do for him now," cried Aren. "We can still make it out of here."

Swing. Dodge. Look to the drain. Repeat. Swing. Dodge. Look to the drain. Nil's legs tired as he waded through the water. His arm was practically numb from swinging the machete. This was a pace he could not keep up. He kept looking to the drain knowing that a slow descent was no longer an option. Though he had reduced the shark's faces to a pulpy mess, it only fueled them to tear him to shreds.

Swing. Dodge. Look to the...

The pattern had finally lost its effectiveness. One of the sharks surged forward, clamping on to his thigh. Nil screamed as he felt the teeth pierce muscle and bone. He had one final move to make, spinning the machete around and driving it straight down into the shark's head, killing it instantly. The move freed Nil but also left him defenseless. Three more sharks advanced towards him. There was only one way he was going to make it out of there alive, one last surge using every final ounce of willpower leaping towards the drain using the flow of the water to carry him the rest of the way.

Enough water had pooled at the bottom of the pipe to cushion his fall. The impact was still painful, further impacting his wounded leg.

"A little help," he said, trying to pull himself through the open door.

Abe began to pull him through the door just as a huge surge of water came pouring down into the pipe. The chamber was flooding with water, the door becoming increasingly difficult to close. Once Nil was safely inside, every able body pushed against the door.

"It's not moving," cried Magdalena.

"Get the other one open," screamed Abe.

"We can't," replied Nil. "The entry door has to be sealed for the other to open. These were designed for high pressure scenarios... underwater entry at deep depths. For one door to open, the other has to be sealed."

"I don't think that's an option anymore," screamed Abe, still pushing on the door.

"Oh god, we're going to drown," said Magdalena, growing increasingly claustrophobic.

"We can climb out," said Abe. "Make our way back out through the Aquarium."

"I'm not exactly in climbing condition," Said Nil, his head barely above the water. "If you go back up that way, the sharks'll get you before the water does."

Abe began to consider his own safety above the mission. He had finally abandoned the concept of leadership and was only concerned with self-preservation. There would be more left behind and the thought became less and less troubling to him with each passing second.

"Wait," said Aren, trying to think.

"Time's not something we have in surplus," said Nil.

"Quiet... quiet..." he replied, scanning the interior, following a series of small copper pipes to the frame of the outer door. "Yes. That's it!"

"What?" said Abe, trying to catch up.

"These systems were designed with a fail-safe," he said, moving to a panel on the far side of the chamber. "We need to get this console open."

Abe rushed across the chamber, pulling out a knife and stabbing it in the space between the panel and the wall. One good thrust and pull tore it away from the hinges. Underneath were a series of wires and switches.

"What now?"

"Give me a second," said Aren, working through a hundred pages of manual in his mind.

"At least tell me what we're looking at."

"The Germans were paranoid," said Aren, beginning to work the wires. "They always built in a remote mechanism to seal off access."

"Like a kill switch?"

"Exactly. Explosives wired into the doors to seal it off in case of emergency."

"I think this qualifies."

"The good news is, I think it's strong enough to blow the door open."

"What's the bad news?"

"It also might be strong enough to kill us," he said, presenting a third more gruesome option for their demise. "If we're lucky, the water will subdue the blast."

"If we're lucky..." said Nil with a sick laugh. "Because we've had such an abundance of it so far."

"We're due," said Abe.

"On the count of three... how do you Americans say? 'Hit the deck'."

Aren held two wires, one in each hand.

"One, two, three."

Nil, Abe, and Magdalena submerged under the water. Aren ducked every body part under the water except for his eyes and hands. Then, he touched the wires together.

The blast was strong enough to blow both doors from the hinges sending a mass of water spraying up to the roof of the chamber. With the chamber door now open, the water flooded into the entryway, carrying everything and everyone with it. Abe shot like a bullet through the narrow entryway, landing hard on the steel grate below. Through his water clogged ears he could hear the sound of a squeaky wheel turning. Someone was sealing the hatch.

CHAPTER TWENTY-THREE

They had finally arrived at his intended destination. For a moment, all he could do was stare down the length of it all. The sound of dripping water echoed down the corridor as it poured from them and onto the grated steel floor.

"I need a headcount," yelled Abe while reaching for his service revolver, wasting no time with managing his limited resources.

One and a half clips of ammunition. Twenty-two bullets. The interior of the submarine was cold and quiet. A submerged tomb that had lain dormant for years. Still, Abe had consistently underestimated the threat level since their arrival. He would not make the same mistake again. This was hostile territory and would be treated as such.

"How many live bodies do I have here?" he yelled as he cocked the gun and aimed it straight ahead. "Do I have my fucking pilot?"

"Yes!" yelled Aren between gasps for air, still exhuming saltwater from his lungs. "I'm here."

"Great. That means we might not die here!" he replied. "Who else?"

"Im here!" said Magdalena, shedding layers of wet clothes.

"God damn sharks!" said Nil, clutching the bloody wound on his leg, the teeth still jutting out from the exposed tissues. "I need some fishing line, a needle and thread, superglue…"

"Get a tourniquet around it, stop the bleeding.

We'll worry about making it pretty later."

"I can get a field dressing on it," replied Magdalena, tying her wet shirt around Nil's leg.

"Try not to die on us, Nil," said Abe. "Aren… you're up."

The last time Aren Brecht had been aboard a vessel like this, he was barely 18. His formative years had been spent in the service of others. This cold, unforgiving relic had been his home. It had seen better days. The seams creaked and water collected around the bolts and rivets holding it together. A sense of nostalgia washed over him. Childhood memories reverberating down the passageway. For Aren, this was a haunted place where he could see the faces of the despicable men his father transported and hear the echoes of old German cavalry songs being sung in the galley.

"What's the first step, Aren?" asked Abe, impatiently waiting for some direction.

"First… we need to get the power going, assuming it's fueled up."

"Let's start there."

Palobar had planned his exit thoroughly. Though neglect had left the ship in less than perfect condition, it had been well maintained before his death. The engine was in working order and the fuel and fluid lines were intact.

"It's seaworthy."

"At least one thing here works."

Aren began the start-up procedures. The old engines began to whir and sputter. The hydraulics creaked as the cylinders began to fire. The old boat still had some life left in it. Nil was hoping the same held true as he tied off the tourniquet holding his mangled leg together.

"This place got a first aid kit?!" he yelled without getting an answer. "If not, a well stocked bar would also work."

Aren ran through the final departure sequence, releasing the moorings and moving the throttle straight ahead. For the first time since starting this journey, Aren experienced a sense of satisfaction. The pleasure of being behind the wheel of the old vessel, the familiar reflexes returning as he pulled back on the yolk.

"How have you been, you delightful old rust bucket?" he asked of her, adjusting the switches on the instrument panel.

Now safely moving towards open water, he surveyed his surroundings. From the corner of his eye, he caught something he had missed in the haste of launch preparation leaning against the generator control levers. Resting inconspicuously in the corner was his father's cane. It was difficult for him to picture his father without it, always gripping it so tightly or using it to gesture when he spoke. This carved wooden apparatus was as much a part of his identity as the tone of his voice or the pale gray color of his perpetually squinting eyes. Aren had never been as close to his father as he would have liked. Jonas had passed on before Aren understood the world, back when he was a boy who still saw his father as the infallible model of righteousness. There were conversations he would like the opportunity to have. Questions a young boy never thinks to ask. Piloting this sub one more time felt like an appropriate way to honor his father who had given so much of himself to its safe passage.

As thrilled as Abe was to be distancing himself from Vaina de la Laga, there was still more to do. He needed to find Palobar's vault. The interior of the sub had been remodeled after its first few voyages. The barracks were stripped of their bunk beds and converted into luxury suites draped with fine linens and stocked with antique furniture. The small galley was now a formal dining room complete with china cabinets and lazy Susans affixed to the table. The gunmetal gray bathroom fixtures had been replaced with fine porcelain, stocked with pearl-handled straight razors and shaving brushes. This highly versatile undersea vessel had been transformed into a claustrophobic pleasure liner.

Abe entered the captain's quarters, the one room where Palobar had conducted heavy renovations. The bookshelves were stocked with his favorite works. The closet lined with an impressive wardrobe that could accommodate any climate. Clearly Palobar had considered his own morality and realized that his reign would end. An exit strategy had been planned. Unfortunately, he had severely overestimated his life expectancy, which was the key flaw in a plan that had several major failings. Vaina de la Laga was no secret in the intelligence community. Everyone knew it was where Palobar would retreat to should push come to shove. It was the scope of his plan that Abe and his peers hadn't considered. The general conceit was that Palobar would go out fighting holed up in this bunker killing as many hired guns as he could, saving that last bullet to take his own life.

That was always the most difficult part of the urban legend of Palobar's vault. No one thought

Palobar possessed a sense of legacy. After Alomena's death, it was almost as if he wanted to die. He had escaped poverty and survived the bloody conflict of the cartel wars. As an analyst, Abe had always believed Palobar was a man with a death wish, the kind of person who had never planned a happily ever after scenario. All the things aboard this ship were the trappings of a man who wanted to survive at any cost.

Logic dictated that Palobar's haul would be in the cargo hold, the only space large enough to hold the kind of riches the stories told of. Abe pulled the lever releasing the door. The room was dark. The lights flickered as the long dormant generators worked their way to full power. He could see the faintest details as his eyes adjusted. Palettes stored in the center of the room wrapped in layers of plastic set up for easy loading and unloading. The only weapon he had left was a small blade tucked into his boot. With it, he split the plastic wrap on the first palette. Inside were hundred dollar bills stacked seven feet high.

Abe went from palette to palette with the gusto of a child on Christmas day unwrapping the presents deposited under the tree. The sounds of the tearing packing materials echoed through the largely empty room. Each one held a different treasure. The second palette housed gold bars. Each of them branded with a number and a seal. The writing was in German. Abe wasn't fluent in the Germanic tongue but had seen enough to pick out the words "Department" and "Treasury".

The third palette contained a series of wooden storage boxes hastily assembled with nails and packing tape. A few quick cuts snapped the loose-fitting framework and spilled the contents onto the floor below. Each box contained circular cardboard mailers. Abe tore the top off of one, sliding out the contents. Inside was a rolled canvas which he carefully unfurled. The painting was a striking portrait. He knew it had to be valuable but lacked the schooling to identify the artist or the era from which it came.

"It's Raphael," said Magdalena, who had managed to enter the room unnoticed due to Abe's celebratory binge. "Portrait of a Young Man."

"What's it worth?" he asked, staring into the bright blues and browns of the painting.

"It's priceless," she replied.

"Everything has a price," he said, looking past the canvas to the vast number of cardboard tubes still unopened. "We might not get what it's worth, but we'll get something for it."

"Why bother? There's enough money in here to make us wealthy enough to not have to worry about moving stolen goods."

"Maybe for you. I plan on wringing every last drop of blood money out of this enterprise."

"That's because you're greedy," said Magdalena.

"It's because I'm a capitalist," he said with a sneer.

"Americans," she snubbed. "Everything's about the bottom dollar."

"Damn right. I didn't go through this gauntlet of nightmares to walk away with a fraction of a fortune."

"Is it just about the balance sheet?" she asked, genuinely curious about his answer. "Does everything have to be reduced to its monetary value?"

"I'm afraid it does," he said without so much as a second thought. "I know where you came from. I've seen the slums you crawled out of. I understand romanticizing Palobar and his lifestyle. Anybody in your position would. How do you not admire someone who came from nothing and achieved all of this. But the thing is, it's just blood money. The house, the zoo, the beautiful trimmings… nothing more than polish. This art, it's blood. Several generations of blood. It was stolen by a bunch of Nazi pricks who brutally murdered the owners, traded away to guarantee safe passage to this humid fucking hell-hole and then bought by a drug lord who made his fortune turning a generation of kids into addicts. Turning those boroughs you toiled into war zones. Everything in here is currency paid for with genocide. Blood money waiting to be cashed in."

The cut was quick, so fast that he saw the first few drops stain the canvas before he felt the pain. He tried to speak, but nothing came out. The priceless canvas was soon covered in blood. Abe turned to see Magdalena holding a razor, one of the pearl-handled ones from the shaving kits in the bathroom.

"...the hell?" he said, only able to vocalize pieces of sentences.

He gripped his hand around the wound, the blood seeping from in between his fingers.

"I'm sorry," she said, backing away from Abe. "This isn't what he would have wanted."

There were so many thoughts going through his head. The loudest being the damning disappointment that he had underestimated her, that his planning and strategy had a fundamental flaw: she was an intangible he hadn't properly factored. This was not a potential scenario he had considered. He tried to quiet the screaming rage and start thinking about survival. In his current state, he was vulnerable. She still stood there with a weapon in her hand watching the blood drain from him. Step one hadn't changed: eliminate potential threats.

His vision was blurry and his strength was fading. Still, he had enough strength for one last throw, flinging his knife across the room. On a good day, with ideal conditions, the blow would have killed her. But his aim was off. The knife landed in her abdomen. A wave of pain washed over her, and she crumpled to the ground, dropping the razor as her hand went limp. Now they were on a level playing field.

CHAPTER TWENTY-FOUR

The knife extended from her stomach like a protruding bone. It hurt when she took each breath. Her initial reaction was to try and pull out the knife. This is natural, the urge to remove the foreign object that has punctured your flesh and muscle. The uninitiated immediately begin to pull and tear at the blade not realizing it's causing more damage than the initial strike. Most revert to instinct not realizing that the item that caused this damage may keep your innards from spilling or is preventing a cut artery from bleeding out.

Magdalena began to pull at the blade handle wincing at every shock it sent through her nervous system. Even the slightest turn was like touching an exposed wire, forcing her to clench up, then go limp with weakness. Abe crawled along the floor, his one hand still clenched around his slit throat. He would use the other to choke the life out of her if he could get close enough. There were a hundred angry expletives he would have hurled at her had he been able to produce words. In his current state he could only exhale guttural moans and gurgling sounds as the blood began to pour from his mouth.

She scurried backwards trying to put some distance between them. Neither of them were moving fast, both crawling slowly across the metal grating of the submarine floor. She looked back to the door which was still barely ajar. With her diminished strength she lacked the ability to budge the heavy door. Every push was a new symphony of pain. Instead, she would have to maneuver through the narrow space. She lay on her back and twisted her body, trying to keep the handle of the knife from scraping against the door or the floor. Her movements were slight and economical, pausing only to look back to see Abe frantically pursuing her with a crazed look on his face: glazed eyes with blood-stained clenched teeth.

Halfway through the door she could feel the tips of his fingers on her ankle trying to get a grip. She kicked like a mule, exerting most of her remaining strength to fight her way through the opening and into the corridor. The pain in her stomach was unbearable, and she was beginning to lose the feeling in her legs. She could go no further, turning her attention to the door waiting for Abe to come crawling through. This was one catastrophe she would not walk away from. To her surprise, no one emerged.

"Was he dead?" she thought between breaths. The sound of her lungs expanding and retracting rung loudly through the inside of her skull. She refused to shift her focus away from the door, still expecting that moment where her bloody and beaten opponent stormed through the opening with a surge of momentum fueled by the adrenaline of his last dying breath.

CHAPTER TWENTY-FIVE

Scorched earth. Not so much a battle strategy as the last possible move to make when all other options have been removed from the table. Even calling it a 'move' or a 'strategy' felt disingenuous. If conflict was a game of chess, employing a scorched earth scenario would be akin to pushing the board off the table and letting the pieces fall where they may. This is the logic of children and those who refuse to accept defeat. If they can't win the game, they will simply ensure there will be no winners.

Abraham was on the verge of defeat. His insides spilled from his wounds, staining everything below his waist. He staggered down the rear corridor trying to will himself from losing consciousness. He had no plan, other than to silence the screaming voices inside his head as he looked for one final act that would ensure he wouldn't be the last person dying on this day. If there was a means to sink the sub, he would find it.

Magdalena had gathered enough strength to get to her feet. She was too fearful to turn her back on the door. Instead, she advanced forward in small steps, leaning her weight in to try and seal off the corridor. She heard a noise in the deep distance. Metal hitting metal. A faint clanging sound coming from the rear of the sub getting louder and louder. She knew it was Abe, no doubt trying to draw her in. It would not work. She would not be lured into his net like a hooked fish. No matter how much she wanted him to die, she would be willing to wait for him to expire before putting herself at further risk.

"What's going on back there?" said Aren over the loudspeaker.

Magdalena looked to the wall where a red light blinked next to a speaker.

"Aren!" she said, pushing the speaker button with one hand while aiming the gun at the other. "It's Magdalena."

"Are you alright?"

"I'm fine," she replied, trying to calm herself.

"Where are you? Where's Abe?"

"We're… I'm… I'm just outside the cargo hold."

"One of the alarms went off on the panel," said Aren, staring at the blinking red light on the panel

"I don't understand?" she said, still staring straight ahead at the gap in the door.

"A rear torpedo hatch has opened," he said. "You don't want to mess around with those."

"There are live torpedoes on this submarine?" she asked.

"No. Of course not. But if one is opened for launch improperly, it could flood the ship."

"We may have a problem," she said realizing that she might not yet be finished with Abe.

The sound of metal clashing against metal was ringing through the rear of the vessel, chiming loudly enough to be heard at the ship's center. Each clang a reminder of the impending doom that faced the handful of survivors.

"What happened back there?" asked Nil, looking down to his mangled leg.

"He went crazy," she replied. "He tried to kill me. I was barely able to get away."

"How much damage could he do back there, Aren?"

"A lot, actually. He could depressurize the aft section. He could sever the interior power supply forcing us to surface, which makes us visible and highly likely to be boarded."

"What aren't you telling us, sweetheart?" asked Nil, looking her dead in the eye. "Why would the guy who brought us all down here on this treasure hunt try to sink the treasure?"

She had no immediate answer, succumbing to the effects of shock. Her body trembled. Her clothes were covered in blood, both hers and his.

"We have to stop him if we want to make it out of here alive, " she said, desperate to keep the remaining survivors focused on stopping Abe.

That was the one truth she was capable of telling, and the only one that mattered.

Nil limped to the back of the submarine, gun in hand. He didn't think Aren could beat a kitten in a wrestling match on a good day and Magdalena was in no condition to fight, not that she would've been much of a fighter even without the knife sticking out of her stomach anyways. He met her a little ways down the corridor.

"I'll be fine," she said, gripping the wound on her belly. "Go take care of Abe. That bastard's going to get us all killed."

Nil nodded and left her to fix her own wounds. Maybe it wasn't the most gentlemanly thing to do, but the three of them had much bigger problems than her injury.

Aren's frantic voice reverberated from the loudspeakers as Nil trudged down the narrow corridor, giving him instructions on where to go to reach the rear torpedo hatch where the presumably grief-crazed Abe was trying to open so that they could all join him in Davy Jones' Locker.

When he reached the hatch, he found Abe trying to turn the massive wheel. Key word being 'trying'. Nil silently wondered why he or Magdalena for that matter was so nervous. Already battered from all the shit he'd been through in the zoo on the surface, Abe was further injured by a huge gash across his throat. Nil could only assume that it had been inflicted by Magdalena in self-defense.

The wound forced Abe to keep one hand around his throat at all times. He was already going to bleed out no matter what. Like fixing holes in a sinking ship, he was only delaying the inevitable. And yet he still tried desperately to open the hatch with his one free hand attached to a shoulder that had been dislocated not so long ago in one last ditch attempt to make sure he didn't have to go to hell alone. And so Nil committed his first and only act of mercy in his whole violent life, placing the barrel of his gun at the base of his skull.

"I'd ask if you had any last words, but it looks like you're all out."

The small caliber .22 bullet buried itself into his skull and stayed there without risk of ricochet. The man who'd once killed and tortured and led men across the world without an ounce of regret dropped to the floor like a sack of potatoes, as dead as all his victims were after he was finished with them. A sad, sad end for a man who had probably never known what real happiness felt like.

Nil limped to the nearest speaker and pressed the

button to contact Aren back in the pilot's seat.

"Abe's dead," he said, bereft of any emotion.

No answer.

"Aren?" Nil asked again, growing worried. "Magdalena? Are you there too? Speak up, I can't hear you."

A knot formed in Nil's stomach. He rushed for the command console and found Aren sitting on the captain's chair with his throat slit from ear to ear. The poor old bastard didn't even stand a chance. He looked to the console and the overwhelming number of gauges and meters. A myriad of numbers and percentages that he lacked the skill to decipher.

"Magdalena," he whispered under his breath before breaking into a string of curse words.

Using up what little remained of his strength, he limped back to the cargo hold. Loose bills were strewn about the floor, the plastic wrap around them having been cut open. Several of the cardboard tubes containing countless canvases were gone. The heavier items remained untouched. He could see a single brick of Nazi gold had been removed. Then, back towards the front of the ship, he could hear a grinding sound.

He worked his way back towards the front of the ship, the condition of his leg deteriorating and making each step more painful. The noise had suddenly stopped, but there were droplets of blood and hundred dollars bills giving him a clear path to follow like a trail of breadcrumbs. They led him to a ladder. He looked up to see Magdalena inside one of the submarine's escape trunks along with whatever treasure she could carry.

"I'm not gonna lie," said Nil, leaning on the ladder

as he lacked the strength to hold himself up, "I'm struggling to put two and two together here. I understand the urge to put a knife in Abe's throat… but Aren? What did that old bastard ever do to you?"

"The old Nazi? The same thing you all did," she said with a grin. "You brought your poison into my country."

"Poison?" replied Nil. "Hate to tell ya' darlin', but in your country, poison was an export."

"Not the drugs. Greed… malice… it's all your people ever brought us. You came into our country, pillaged our resources and turned our suffering into profit."

It was almost enough to make Nil laugh.

"There are two kinds of people in this world," said Nil with a sneer. "The unwashed masses yearning to be free and the people stepping on their necks. Which side do you think your boy Palobar was on?"

"He was far from perfect," she said, "but he gave back to his people. Fed us, clothed us… He never forgot where he came from."

"Because he drove through the shit-covered boroughs throwing out handfuls of money pretending to be Robin Hood?" said Nil, still amused by her portrayal of the infamous kingpin."

"Because he gave us hope that one day we could control our own destiny and wrestle our land back from the babeco."

"So here's what's going to happen," said Nil between short breaths. "You're gonna get out of that escape trunk and come on down here."

"Why would I do that?" she replied.

"Because I'm guessing it'll take me less time to raise my gun and fire than it will for you to close that heavy hatch. Cause if you did, you would have already shut the damn thing."

"You're right."

"So why don't you put both hands where I can see them and slowly come on down so we can end this."

Magdalena slowly brought her hands into view.

"You really thought you were going to make it out of here?" asked Nil.

"I still do, she replied, showing her right hand which clutched a gold brick.

She loosened her grip and let gravity do the rest, the brick plummeting down straight towards Nil. His eyes went wide as he struggled to aim his gun upwards, the gold bar plummeting downwards. He frantically pulled the trigger, the bullets ricocheting off the curvature of the entry point. Magdalena reached out and pulled with all her might to close the hatch, seeing the heavy gold bar make impact on the bridge of Nil's nose and send him crumpling to the floor. She used her remaining strength to seal the latch and pull the release lever.

Nil lay on the floor of the submarine, a fresh stream of blood pouring from each nostril. The man whose own nickname marked him as worthless, watched helplessly as the escape trunk launched, causing the ship to tremble. This is where he would spend his final moments; alone on a forgotten ship with not even the skies to see him off as he returned to nothing.

Chapter Twenty-Six

Her skin felt so wonderfully warm, the bright sun having dried her as she slept. The light flooded into her eyes as she attempted to force herself from slumber. There were sharp pains whenever she tried to move her arms and legs. Even twisting her neck from side to side took a great deal of effort.

She pulled herself up and began to scan the water, looking for anything else that may have surfaced. All she could see was the still blue water and the shimmers of a setting sun offering a picturesque view. Part of her remained convinced that someone else would emerge from the water and that her fight was not quite over.

This was all part of her process. Burning through the panic and paranoia before eventually forcing herself to make a plan. Scraping together whatever pieces were at her disposal to try and find a way to survive one more day. Far from home, adrift in unfriendly waters and holding on to a tiny sliver of hope that might lead her one step closer to freedom.

The End

Check out other great

Cryptid Novels!

J.H. Moncrieff

RETURN TO DYATLOV PASS

In 1959, nine Russian students set off on a skiing expedition in the Ural Mountains. Their mutilated bodies were discovered weeks later. Their bizarre and unexplained deaths are one of the most enduring true mysteries of our time. Nearly sixty years later, podcast host Nat McPherson ventures into the same mountains with her team, determined to finally solve the mystery of the Dyatlov Pass incident. Her plans are thwarted on the first night, when two trackers from her group are brutally slaughtered. The team's guide, a superstitious man from a neighboring village, blames the killings on yetis, but no one believes him. As members of Nat's team die one by one, she must figure out if there's a murderer in their midst—or something even worse—before history repeats itself and her group becomes another casualty of the infamous Dead Mountain.

Gerry Griffiths

CRYPTID ZOO

As a child, rare and unusual animals, especially cryptid creatures, always fascinated Carter Wilde. Now that he's an eccentric billionaire and runs the largest conglomerate of high-tech companies all over the world, he can finally achieve his wildest dream of building the most incredible theme park ever conceived on the planet... CRYPTID ZOO. Even though there have been apparent problems with the project, Wilde still decides to send some of his marketing employees and their families on a forced vacation to assess the theme park in preparation for Opening Day. Nick Wells and his family are some of those chosen and are about to embark on what will become the most terror-filled weekend of their lives—praying they survive. STEP RIGHT UP AND GET YOUR FREE PASS... TO CRYPTID ZOO

@severedpress
/severedpress

Check out other great

Cryptid Novels!

Ian Faulkner

CRYPTID

Be careful what you look for. You might just find it.1996. A group of 14 students walked into the trackless virgin forests of Graham Island, British Columbia for a three-day hike. They were never seen again. 2019. An American TV crew retrace those students' steps to attempt to solve a 23-year-old mystery.A disparate collection of characters arrives on the island. But all is not as it seems. Two of them carry dark secrets. Terrible knowledge that will mean death for some – but a fighting chance of survival for others. In the hidden depths of the forests – man is on the menu. Some mysteries should remain unsolved...

Eric S. Brown

LOCH NESS HORROR

The Order of the Eternal Light, a secret organization have foretold the end of the human race. In order to save all humanity, agents of the Order must locate the Loch Ness Monster and obtain a sample of its blood for within in it is the key to stopping the apocalypse but finding the monster will be no easy task.

Check out other great

Cryptid Novels!

P.K. Hawkins

THE CRYPTID FILES

Fresh out of the academy with top marks, Agent Bradley Tennyson is expecting to have the pick of cases and investigations throughout the country. So he's shocked when instead he is assigned as the new partner to "The Crag," an agent well past his prime. He thinks the assignment is a punishment. It's anything but.Agent George Crag has been doing this job for far longer than most, and he knows what skeletons his bosses have in the closet and where the bodies are buried. He has pretty much free reign to pick his cases, and he knows exactly which one he wants to use to break in his new young partner: the disappearance and murder of a couple of college kids in a remote mountain town.Tennyson doesn't realize it, but Crag is about to introduce him to a world he never believed existed: The Cryptid Files, a world of strange monsters roaming in the night. Because these murders have been going on for a long time, and evidence is mounting that the murderer may just in fact be the legendary Bigfoot.

Gerry Griffiths

DOWN FROM BEAST MOUNTAIN

A beast with a grudge has come down from the mountain to terrorize the townsfolk of Porterville. The once sleepy town is suddenly wide awake. Sheriff Abel McGuire and game warden Grant Tanner frantically investigate one brutal slaying after another as they follow the blood trail they hope will eventually lead to the monstrous killer. But they better hurry and stop the carnage before the census taker has to come out and change the population sign on the edge of town to ZERO.

www.ingramcontent.com/pod-product-compliance
Lightning Source LLC
Chambersburg PA
CBHW061242170626
46809CB00007B/2797
* 9 7 8 1 9 2 2 5 5 1 6 7 2 *